My beloved former President Carter,
I wish you Abundance JOY and Success.

Sept 24, 2021

Secret Boyfriend

A Novel…Inspired by a True Story

D1121208

Paul Noor

ISBN: 978-0-9885283-4-5

Contents

Acknowledgements

There are so many individuals and groups of people that I should acknowledge in my novel, but I limited it to only three:

1) To my beautiful Filipina ex-wife, for twelve years of wonderful memories together. I hope one day you will accept my offer to become each other's BEST friend. I still miss you babe…**HUG!**

2) To all the people who gave me feedback, especially Filipina ladies living in the Philippines. They gave me constructive recommendations and steered me in the right direction.

3) To the staff of Starbucks Coffee in Las Vegas, USA. While writing this novel, I would go there every day at 5 a.m., right after they opened the store. I was their first customer, and I would get my favorite venti dark-roast coffee. I would then go to my favorite table in a corner with a tall window.

I would take my laptop and coffee, and from that tall window, I would fly to space. I found a rock in space above Las Vegas. I would go there and sit on that rock and write this novel. I wanted to write this novel in space, where there are no distractions—and where there is no hatred—so that I could let my imagination loose and go wild into uncharted territory. I wanted this novel to be out of the box, or I better say, out of this planet.

If you feel my novel has too much fantasy or I might have been hallucinating, it's because my novel was written on a rock in space. Unfortunately, I cannot give you the location of that rock because it's my hiding place for my future writings, especially my next novel, *Secret Boyfriend, Part II.*

Paul Noor
From a rock in space above Las Vegas, USA
www.SecretBoyfriend.com

From the Author:

This is a novel, only inspired by a true story. "Introduction" is true, but the rest is a novel, it's fiction, not true. Mark was never the Mafia Boss in Las Vegas and never strangled anyone. And Dr. Ann Ruby, my lovely Filipina wife in the novel, doesn't live in Las Vegas. I wish she did! Those characters don't exist in real life…only in my novel.

My intention was to turn my sad story into an entertaining and inspiring novel with **FORGIVENESS** at its core, and with a sweet ending of **Uniting Broken Relationships**.

Remember, this novel was written on a rock in space above Las Vegas, USA. Fasten your seat belt because it's a wild ride. Expect some bumps and bruises, but otherwise, I hope you will be entertained and inspired by this novel and delighted with the unexpected happy ending.

Names have been changed to protect their identities.

If you decide to read this novel, make sure to read it to the end, because the icing on the cake is in the second half.

Introduction

The True Story

To My Beautiful Filipina Ex-Wife,

Sweetheart, ever since I caught you with your Secret Boyfriend in his white Mercedes convertible, you went into hiding and have ignored my many attempts to be friends.

Twelve years ago, when I first met you in Davao City, Philippines, you instantly stole my heart and I immediately fell in love with you. I decided to sponsor you, bring you to the USA, introduce you to a better life, and make you my princess.

1

For twelve years, you were the TRUE LOVE OF MY LIFE! You were my everything. You were my whole world. The rest of the world was secondary.

My greatest joy was seeing you SHINE. If anyone would say anything bad about you, I would finish them.

For two years, from mid-2017 to mid-2019, I devoted my life to you like a humble servant, helping you with college classes, passing exams, and getting a license, a respectable full-time job in the healthcare industry, and a new car. I also helped you become a US citizen so that you could get your US passport and become independent.

I knew that when a few of your close married Filipina friends became independent, they ran away with their Secret Boyfriends, but I didn't care. I said I would give my ultimate being to melt your heart, as I believed you would be my lovely wife to the last day of my life—even though the odds were against me.

In the end, your humble servant lost the battle!!! You completely changed, and that heartbreak sent me directly to the emergency room of the hospital. I had a stroke, twice, but I fought back—alone— and I survived both times. I am now writing this novel from my hospital bed.

Instead of paying me back with your love and support so that I could get back on my feet too, you ran away with your Secret Boyfriend in his white Mercedes convertible and left me hopeless in my red Honda Civic.

But I still love you, babe. Please come back, or at least visit me in the hospital, or just reply to my text. It's sooooo painful to live in our small apartment without you.

Because of the stroke, my right arm is still numb. I am praying that you will come back to massage it for me. I miss you sooooo much, my ONLY love.
Please come back…
Please…
Pleeeeease…
Pleeeeeeeeeease…

Secret Boyfriend — Paul Noor

The Novel

Chapter One

The Rush to the Hospital

The ambulance raced through the city of Las Vegas,
just past the famous, iconic sign on Las Vegas
Boulevard that says, "Welcome to Fabulous Las
Vegas, Nevada." There was a long line of tourists
waiting to take pictures with it.

It arrived at my apartment building, which was on
Las Vegas Boulevard. I was lying on the couch in the
family room of my small, messy, second-floor
apartment. I had left the door unlocked for the
paramedics.

When they came inside, one paramedic asked me,
"Mr. Noor, what is the problem?"

I said, "My right arm is numb, also half of my face. I believe I had a stroke."

She then asked me, "How long have you had these symptoms?"

I said, "Since last night, more than twelve hours ago."

She said, "Why did you wait that long? When a stroke happens, you should call 911 immediately. If you go to the hospital quickly, sometimes they can reverse it. I hope they can do that for you too."

In my messy apartment, there was one thing that caught her attention. It was the beautiful wedding portrait of my wife, Cristina, and me. At the bottom, it read, "Paul and Cristina are FOREVER."

The lady looked at the picture and said, "You have a beautiful wife. Where is she to take care of you?"

I burst into tears and said, "She is my beautiful Filipina wife. When she became independent and received her US passport, she ran away with her Secret Boyfriend in his white Mercedes convertible and left me hopeless in my red Honda Civic, but I still love her. She is my world. She is my everything. I want her back."

The lady didn't want to get into my private life, so she didn't ask me any more questions.

They put me on the stretcher and took my personal items. I said, "Please take that portrait too. I want it to be with me." She took it and gave it to me, and I held it on my chest to be close to my heart. I was hoping that she would come back...to massage my right arm.

They took me out of the apartment, locked the door, took me downstairs, and put me in the back of their ambulance. They drove out of the complex, turned on the siren and flashing emergency lights, and drove toward the hospital.

While the ambulance was racing through traffic, I could hear the paramedic talking to the emergency room of the hospital, saying, "We just picked up a stroke patient. He is in bad shape. He said he had the stroke more than twelve hours ago. His right arm and half of his face are numb; he has no feeling in them.

"Please get everything ready quickly. Hopefully, they can reverse his stroke. He is very depressed and crying. Apparently, his Filipina wife ran away with her Secret Boyfriend, and he cannot handle the pain. We will be there in less than ten minutes."

The emergency room staff prepared everything quickly and were ready for our arrival. Dr. Stacy was the first person to check my condition. She immediately did some basic tests to see if I had a stroke, then sent me for more tests.

After a few hours, Dr. Stacy came to me and said, "We still don't know what happened to you. It seems to me, you are under super tension and stress, and that could have been the reason for what happened.

"We are going to keep you here for another twenty-four hours and do more tests to find out exactly what happened to you. Those tests will tell us if you had a stroke or not. Someone will be here to transfer you in a wheelchair to a different room."

Before she left, I said, "Dr. Stacy, can I have a notepad and pen, please?"

She said, "Sure…" She gave me a notepad and a pen from her pocket, then smiled and left. I then started writing this novel on that notepad in my hospital bed.

Chapter Two

I Became the BEST Secret Boyfriend

After writing the first few pages of my novel while in my hospital bed, I felt so depressed and broken.

I could see no light at the end of the tunnel. Everything was completely dark and black in my life. I felt like I was at the bottom of a black hole.

I forced myself to get out of my bed in the hospital room and walk down the corridor to a large picture window. Looking at the sky, everything seemed dark to me. There was no life, and if there was, it had no meaning to me.

I had been betrayed so badly by the lady I loved and had helped sooo much. She was my whole world. She was my everything. Life without Cristina had no meaning to me. That moment was the end of my life.

Then the phone rang. I wasn't sure if I should answer it, but I did. It was a lady with a loving voice. She said, "Paul, this is Angelina, your wife's younger sister."

"Angelina, how are you? I haven't spoken to you in a while. It's good to hear your voice," I replied.

She then said, "I heard about what my sister did to you…running away with her Secret Boyfriend. I was devastated…so brutal. But don't feel alone. The reason for my call is to let you know that I am one hundred percent on your side, and I will love you forever."

Wow…love me FOREVER?!

She then continued, "I have always had a crush on you and I knew that you liked me too, but I couldn't express my feelings because both of us were married. Now that Cristina has run away, I couldn't be happier.

"I want to be with you. I've wished I was with you for the past twelve years. Paul, I love you sooo much. This is the moment I have been waiting for. Will you be my Secret Boyfriend?"

I said, "Angelina, but you are married to Mark and have a ten-year-old son!"

She answered, "Yes, I am married, but I want to escape. It's like being in prison with him. I ONLY want to be with you. Paul, would you be my Secret Boyfriend...Please? You have no idea how much I love you...Pleeeeease?"

I could not believe what I was hearing. Was this real, or was I on too much medication from the doctor?

She then said, "Paul, can we meet tomorrow morning after I drop my son off at school? I'll text you the address of a shopping center near the school. I'll be driving a new, red Mercedes convertible. Call me when you get to the shopping center. Is nine a.m. good for you?"

I said, "Yes, sure. I will be there at nine a.m."

Suddenly, light appeared. The sky turned blue, and I felt like the happiest man in the world. I was going to be Angelina's Secret Boyfriend. Heaven on Earth!

I whispered, "Cristina, thank you very much for running away."

I whistled and danced back to my room to pick up my stuff and leave the hospital. I saw a few nurses and staff sitting on my bed, reading the first few pages of my novel, which I had just written on a notepad. They were crying and feeling bad for me.

I went to them with excitement and ultimate happiness and screamed, "I just became the Secret Boyfriend. Yes, I just became the Secret Boyfriend. My wife's married younger sister just asked me to become her Secret Boyfriend. Yes…Yes…Yes…I am the happiest man in the world!"

One of the ladies wrote her cell number on a piece of paper and said, "I'd like you to be my Secret Boyfriend too. Would you consider me if it doesn't work out with your wife's sister?"

I said, "Sure…I will," and I took her number.

A lady with a wheelchair was in the room too. I asked, "Who are you?!"

She replied, "Mr. Noor, I am here to take you to another room."

I said, "Take me to another room in a wheelchair?! NO WAY!!!"

I grabbed the lady by both hands and guided her into the wheelchair. While singing and dancing, I pushed her out of the room and through the lobby. She could not believe what was happening.

In the lobby, the doctor who had treated me was talking to her colleagues. They were shocked to see me so happy and vibrant. "Isn't he your stroke patient?" I overheard one ask.

He then continued, "How did you treat him so fast? This is incredible!!! You need to teach and train other doctors about treating stroke patients!" My doctor stood there with her mouth open.

At my car, I helped the lady out of the wheelchair. She said, "That was the most joyful ride of my life. You are sooo fun, Paul! Would you be my Secret Boyfriend too?" She also gave me her cell number.

As I was getting into my car, another lady who worked in the hospital ran up to me. She had our portrait in her hands and said, "Mr. Noor...Mr. Noor, you forgot to take the portrait of you and your beautiful Filipina wife, Cristina!"

I said, "You can have it...I found a better one!"

I got into my car, drove to my apartment, and showered. I was excited to start fresh and meet my new LOVE, Angelina. I was determined to impress her and be the BEST Secret Boyfriend in the world.

MEETING ANGELINA AT MANILA AIRPORT

First, let me tell you why Angelina had a crush on me. Well, let me be honest with you, I had a crush on her as well, but I never expressed it openly. It was a love affair that was never discussed and no one knew about it, except for Angelina and me.

The story goes back twelve years. At that time, she was living in Manila. After I met Cristina in Davao City, Philippines, on my way back to the United States, Angelina stopped by at Manila Airport to meet me. She wanted to approve me as an incoming family member. We spent a couple of hours together.

The moment I met her, I felt different. Angelina was full of love. She was caring and very romantic. That was something I was looking for. Cristina was a little rough, not very caring, and I couldn't feel her love, even though I loved her.

Angelina and I went to a restaurant at the airport to eat something. We ordered the food, and while I was eating, she took a napkin and cleaned the corner of my mouth. That was a touch that I will never forget. Cristina had never done such a thing, nor did I think she ever would.

In that moment, Angelina stole my soul as well as my heart; I could get neither back. I was convinced that I was marrying the wrong sister, but it was too late. I was too involved with Cristina, and Angelina was also involved with another American potential husband.

On the plane coming back to the United States, I spent the whole time thinking about how to switch these two sisters.

MEETING ANGELINA AFTER TWELVE YEARS

When Angelina called me, it was like heaven opened for me. I felt like I was getting my love back. My real love.

The next day, after she dropped her son off at school, we both parked at the same shopping center, and I got in Angelina's sexy, new, red Mercedes convertible.

WOW…I had never ridden in a car like that, and now, the true love of my life was picking me up for a date in one. I thought I had died and gone to heaven.

She drove toward the outside of town to a secluded park with a view of the hills. It was sooooo romantic…the two of us sitting on the bench… under the shade of a tree…viewing the hills in the distance. No one could see us…it was just the two of us.

She brought coffee, cookies, and some fruit. We sat and started talking. She wore a beautiful dress, which was a little exotic for going out to the park and to comfort a depressed and broken family member. It was like she had dressed up for a romantic date.

While we were talking, she slowly touched my hand, like a comforting family member, but we both knew that it was different.

Angelina and my wife had not spoken to each other for about ten years. They hated each other. They were like two rivals. They had two different personalities. My wife was rough, and Angelina was loving, caring, and SWEET!!!

Angelina said, "My marriage with Mark is not going well at all. My husband is a heavy drinker. He is a businessman and all he thinks about is money, money, and even more money."

She continued and said, "Paul, I wanted to escape from my marriage, but I didn't know how. I am glad we got back together after twelve years. I have been looking for an opportunity to escape. I think you are the opportunity."

I said to myself, *What?! I am the opportunity!!!*

Wow!!! I couldn't believe what I was hearing. She was definitely telling me that she was available for me. And, of course, I was as available as I could get, and ready to jump on any opportunity, especially on sexy, sweet, and HOT Angelina.

She then said, "When we got married, Mark didn't have anything. He made all his fortune after that. We did not sign a prenuptial agreement, so if we get divorced, I will get half the family fortune, which is substantial."

Was she thinking about marrying me? Just a few days ago, when my wife ran away, I was so depressed and felt like I was at the bottom of a black hole, and now this!!!

I knew there was an attraction between us, but I didn't know it was this strong. Suddenly, my life changed completely.

At the same time, I tried my hardest to control my feelings toward Angelina, even though I could feel she was ready for more. I was scared to go too fast. I had real love for her, heart to heart and not just sexual, although I felt that she was ready to jump on me, even on that park bench.

That was the most enjoyable date I have ever had. No wonder we were attracted to each other. I never had such a romantic date with my wife. Right then, I decided to focus on my real love, my wife's married, sweet, good-looking, hot...hot...I mean...HOT younger sister, Angelina.

Our first date, which was supposed to last for about thirty minutes, was a lot longer. We stayed in that corner of the park for a few hours. We were talking, laughing, and enjoying each other. No physical touching, except Angelina kept touching my hand and a few times went to my elbow deep inside my shirt. Besides that, it was pure love.

At lunchtime, she went to her car and brought out the lunch she had prepared for us. Obviously, she had expected our date would last longer than I had. On that date, she stole my heart completely.

I was broken physically, emotionally, and financially. I didn't mind her stealing my heart AT ALL! What else could I lose?! I couldn't go lower.

On that date, Angelina became my new and ONLY love of my life, and she wanted me to be her Secret Boyfriend. I was determined to perform my best and to impress her.

At the end, we decided to see each other again. Angelina said, "How about tomorrow?"

Wow…she was HOT and wanted more, and of course, I didn't mind, so I said, "YES!"

She bought one of those cell phones with no name attached to it so her husband couldn't detect it. She told her husband that she was doing lots of volunteer work for the school and didn't want them to have her personal cell number. Mark believed her lie.

She put a private password on it so her husband could not check it. That cell phone was only for us to text, call, or video chat. She was a lot more serious about being with me than I was with her. Again, I didn't mind it AT ALL.

That night, our private chatting began. She told her husband that a parent of a kid in school needed her help, and she had to go to the living room and chat with them.

Mark was so drunk that he didn't mind at all. She relaxed on the couch and started chatting with me. Being single and lonely, I was truly enjoying my new relationship with Angelina.

The next morning, right after dropping her son off, we met again at the parking lot of the shopping center, and I jumped in her sexy car. This time, she drove a little further, to a mountainside. A river was running and people were walking or jogging along it.

Again, she found a secluded area. I said, "Angelina, there is no bench here to sit on."

She said, "Don't worry. I came prepared." She brought out two picnic chairs, homemade Filipino food, and a small tent for us to relax in for the afternoon.

I said silently, *I better get ready for her plan. It will be hot...hot...I mean...HOT.* And I was ready to enjoy every second of it.

We sat watching the river and started talking. Again, she slowly extended her hand and held mine. That was when I felt that I was officially her Secret Boyfriend, and I was ready to go ALL IN.

We then went inside the tent to relax. She turned on her side toward me while holding my hand, then started talking to me and touching my hair and face. She was ready, and I decided not to waste any time.

I touched her hair, her beautiful eyebrows, her face, then started kissing her and playing with her body. Suddenly, everything erupted out of control, and we started calling each other "babe," "my love," and "sweetheart."

I am not sure if her attraction toward me was because of the true love between us, or if she was using me to escape from her husband, or maybe she wanted to get revenge on her sister by having sex with me, or maybe all the above. But I was ready for her to get as much revenge as she wanted. Every moment of that revenge was SWEET.

We had twelve years of catching up to do. We both realized that we had married the wrong people and it was time to enjoy every moment of being together.

HER HUSBAND CAUGHT US

After a few hours of romantic time together, we left our isolated place near the river. It was time for Angelina to pick her son up from school. There was no phone reception, so we'd had absolutely no interruption. It was only the two of us.

In the car going back, we laughed and enjoyed each other…just like new high-school sweethearts. We didn't care about anything in the world. It was sooo sweet.

While I was sitting close and playing with her hair, a policeman on a motorcycle pulled up next to us. He looked at us intently. Apparently, he was jealous of us being so in love. Suddenly, he turned on his flashing lights and siren and guided us to the side of the road.

He parked right behind us and walked up. He asked Angelina for her driver's license and insurance card. While the officer was looking at Angelina's name, I had one hand on her leg and my other hand rubbing her arm for support. The officer saw me very clearly and realized that we were inseparable.

The officer said, "Your husband called us and said you had disappeared, and he couldn't find you. We have been looking for your car all over the Las Vegas area."

He then asked in a suspicious way, "Who is this asshole? Your Secret Boyfriend? Give your husband a call. He said he loves you sooo much and is eagerly waiting for you."

Suddenly, I froze like a deer in headlights. I moved my hands slowly away from Angelina. It was obvious that she was in big trouble.

When we got closer to town, where there was phone reception, Angelina saw several voice messages and texts from her husband and the school.

She said, "This is very unusual and has never happened in the past." She parked her car in the parking lot of a gas station and started reading the texts and listening to the voicemails. She then said, "Babe, we are in BIG, BIG trouble."

She said, "My son wasn't feeling well at school and vomited. The school nurse couldn't find me, so she called my husband. He had to leave work and take him home. He has been looking desperately for me."

Suddenly, Angelina screamed with joy and said, "I got it…I got it…I know what to do. I know exactly what to do."

I asked, "You got what?!"

She said, "I came up with a brilliant idea of what to say to my husband. Let me handle it."

She sent this text to her husband: "Babe, there is a big family emergency. Paul was going to commit suicide. But don't worry. I helped him. He is okay now."

Mark replied, "What??? Suicide??? Is he okay now? For sure?"

Angelina replied, "Yes, babe, he is okay. We got so lucky. I am coming home to tell you what happened." She then dropped me off at the shopping-center parking lot and went directly home.

When Angelina got home, she started crying and jumped into Mark's arms and said, "Sweetheart, we have a family crisis."

Mark hugged and kissed her and forgot about his anger.

Angelina said, "Babe, sorry that you had to go to the school to pick up our son."

Mark said, "Don't worry at all. Paul's situation is much more important. Tell me what happened."

Angelina said, "Paul called me this morning and was sooo depressed about my sister running away with her Secret Boyfriend. He said he doesn't want to live anymore. Sweetheart, you are a busy man, I love you sooo much, and I didn't want you to get involved."

Mark raised his voice and said, "What do you mean? You didn't want me to get involved?! Paul is a dear member of our family. Our son calls him Daddy Paul. Why didn't you ask me to help?"

Angelina said, "I decided to handle it myself because you are so busy with your work and supporting our family. My nasty sister took advantage of Paul's kindness, and after she became independent, she ran away. Cristina is such a heartless thief. That's why I don't talk to her. She is a disease in our family."

"So, what did you do, sweetheart?" Mark asked eagerly.

"I told him, 'Please, don't commit suicide. Mark and I love you sooo much. Let's meet after I drop my son off at school and go out and talk.' I thought the best idea would be to drive him out of town, to the river by the mountainside, and let him release his tension by looking at the river, fish, birds, and be calmed by nature.

"I wanted to keep it top secret because I didn't want Paul to get embarrassed about you knowing that he wanted to kill himself. Paul is a good man and has pride. I wanted to help him in a respectful manner. Unfortunately, there was no phone reception in that area. That's why I couldn't call you."

Mark said, "What a brilliant idea. I am sooo proud of you. Honey, you are an angel for saving his life. For all these years, I didn't know that you have such a big heart for helping people. In this case, you actually saved his life."

Mark then said, "Babe, I don't think we should let Paul live alone. We have a guest room in our home. Let's invite him to come and live with us, at least temporarily, until he finds a loving, sweet, caring, and loyal Filipina lady like YOU. Let me call and invite him."

Angelina then said, "Honey, sorry that you had to go to the school. Tell me what happened."

Mark said, "Sweetheart, don't even talk about that. I handled everything. Paul's situation is a lot more important."

Angelina played her role so brilliantly that Mark had forgotten about why he was mad in the first place.

Mark then said, "Sweetheart, my baby, you brought tears to my eyes. What an angel...I know that you are a good Filipina family lady, but I never saw this side of you before.

"I was so busy expanding my business and building a good retirement for us that, at night, I wanted only

26

to come home, collapse on the couch, and drink to numb my pain. I completely missed the angel who was living with me.

"I love you, sweetheart, and I want to help Paul, too. What Cristina did to him was so nasty. Not only did she betray Paul, but she betrayed our whole family. Paul is a good man. We are both going to help him."

Angelina, of course, didn't want Mark to get involved. This was something that she wanted to handle privately with me.

Mark continued, "Sweetheart, why don't we invite Paul to live in our guest room? It has a full bathroom and a small office. He will have his own privacy yet won't be alone, and he can enjoy your delicious Filipino food. I don't want him to be alone in his apartment."

Mark called me and made the offer. I was shocked and really surprised by his generosity. I said, "Mark, thank you very much for your kindness. I wasn't expecting it. I accept your offer and will stay at your home tonight and see how it goes."

They lived in a beautiful house, like a mansion, in a gated community surrounded by other mansions in an exclusive neighborhood in Las Vegas. I had heard that they were doing well, but I didn't know that they were doing this well!

After eating Angelina's delicious Filipino food, Mark started drinking. Angelina said, "He drinks until he passes out. This is his way to numb his pain. He has one mission in life and that is to make money, money, and even more money."

After only a couple of drinks, Mark turned to me. "You're in the real-estate business. Right, Paul?"

I said, "Yes, I am."

He then said, "Paul, you seem to be an intelligent, persistent, and hard-working person. In addition to our construction business, we are also in the land-development business. We buy land, develop it or change the zoning, then sell it."

He then continued, "I'm getting so busy that I don't have time to run it. Would you be interested in running the land-development department for me? You seem to be a very qualified person. I am sure you will do a GREAT job.

"I will give you a fixed salary plus commission. With your talent and dedication, it will be a very lucrative package. What do you think, Paul?"

I could not believe what I had heard. I was so broken financially and mentally, my wife had run away, and I was practically homeless. The offer was so unreal. What a kind and generous man!

I said, "Mark, I would love to be a part of your organization and take it to a higher level."

Mark said, "Good! You are a positive man. I love what you said about taking it to a higher level. You are hired! Welcome aboard, my brother-in-law."

He really liked what I said about taking the company to a higher level. He immediately saw money, money, and even more money.

Then he added, "Oh, I forgot something. We'll buy you a brand-new luxury car. I want you to look successful. It will be good for your confidence and for our company, too. What car do you like, Paul? Regular, convertible? What color?"

Shocked, I said, "That w-w-w-w-would be a-a-a-a-awesome. How about a w-w-w-w-white M-M-M-M-Mercedes c-c-c-c-convertible?" Then I could compete with my wife's Secret Boyfriend.

He then said, "I will take care of it for you tomorrow morning. You can go to the dealership and pick out the one you like."

I said, "Mark, thank you very much for your generosity. I'll make sure that you get your investment back in many folds."

Mark replied, "I have no doubt about it."

Angelina brought Mark another cocktail and said, "Honey, why don't you relax and have another drink? I will take our new guest to his room and show him around." Angelina wanted her husband so drunk that he wouldn't wake up until the morning.

She took me to the guest room and carefully explained, "Paul, there are security cameras everywhere in this home except in the guest room. Mark can check everything on his cell phone.

"You must be very, very careful. He is also a very jealous man. If he sees something going on between us, it could be the end of your life, and maybe mine too."

We returned to the family room. Mark had passed out. Angelina helped him to go to bed, then came back to the family room where I was. We went outside and sat by their pool, which had an astonishing view of the city.

As we sat next to the pool, she said, "Paul, this is my life every night. There is no romance in our marriage and no romantic sex. And when there is, he looks at it as a business transaction, thinking about how he can profit from the energy he is using while having sex. When he is done, he turns his back to me and goes to sleep. He uses sex with me as a sleeping pill."

She then continued, "I really want to get out of this marriage. There is no excitement, no romance, no love. He likes me, but he treats me like a Filipina maid. He wants to keep me in the kitchen to cook, in bed for sex, and at home to clean the house and take care of our son.

"When I came to America, it was my dream to go to nursing school, but he refused. He was afraid that when I graduated and got my US passport, I would run away like your wife. Now I feel useless, but I am entitled to half of his fortune.

"I really want to escape from this marriage. I didn't know how until you came back into my life. Now, I don't want to lose this opportunity. I want you to be my Secret Boyfriend and to help me escape, and hopefully, we will live together FOREVER."

She then said, "When I heard that you helped my sister to go to college and become independent, I became very jealous. I wished you were my husband.

"When my sister ran away, I couldn't have been happier. This was the opportunity of my life, and I immediately asked you to become my Secret Boyfriend. I want you to help me go to college, become a nurse, and gain my independence, too."

She added, "My sister never loved you. I know that for a fact. Before coming to America as your wife, she told me she was marrying you to get out of her hard life in Davao City.

"As soon as she got her education and US passport, she planned to run away with her Secret Boyfriend. She only used you for your kindness to become independent.

"But I've loved you ever since we met at Manila Airport twelve years ago. I still love you, even more than before. I have always said that I wished I'd married you. I love you sooo much, and I want to be with you to the last day of my life.

"If we get married, I won't sign any prenuptial agreement. That means that if, God forbid, we got divorced, you would be entitled to part of my fortune. That is how much I love and trust you. I really love you, Paul. What do you think, my love? It is my dream to change my last name to yours and make it Angelina Noor…I really love you, Paul."

I could not believe what I was hearing. Just a few days ago, I was a broken man, depressed, couldn't get out of bed, and now this!!! But it was a scary and complicated situation. Just this morning, I was lying down in the tent with Mark's wife, playing with her hair, body, and kissing her.

Tonight, Mark offered me a generous package and treated me like his younger brother, even inviting me to sleep in their home. Now, his lovely Filipina wife wanted me to marry her, with all the fortune that she would get after divorcing him.

It was too overwhelming and hard to digest. The whole thing felt so un-real, like a novel written on a rock in space.

I thought the best thing would be to sleep and hopefully wake up fresh with a new plan in the morning.

I said, "Angelina, I need to go to my room and sleep." She turned off the light in the pool area and came with me. We entered my room and she made sure everything was right and comfortable for me.

She then closed the door and gave me a big hug and started kissing me. I said, "No, please don't do it. Not here...Please...It's dangerous."

She said, "Don't worry, there is no camera in this guest room, and he is drunk anyway."

I said, "Please, you have to stop it. We will continue it tomorrow. Please go to your room." I opened the door for her and she left.

Angelina didn't sleep next to her husband; instead, she slept on the couch in the family room. She started texting and video-chatting with me on her secret cell phone. Finally, she let me sleep.

In the middle of the night, there was a knock on my door. I was very scared. Was it Mark coming to kill me? I slowly opened the door, ready for the worst. It was Angelina.

I asked her, "What are you doing here? I told you not to come to my room."

She said, joking, "I came here to make sure you are not going to commit suicide!" She then laughed lightly.

I said, "Get OUT of here! Go back to sleep. I'll see you in the morning." I shut and locked the door. Luckily, she did not come back.

When I was in the guest room alone, I saw something that really scared me. There was a portrait of Mark with the chief of police. At the bottom, it said, "With my buddy, Chief Johnson."

Why would the chief of police want to be buddies with such a huge land developer? There was definitely corruption here. The chief had to be neutral to everyone, not buddy only to the big one. This confirmed my suspicions that I was in a dangerous situation.

I have never been sooo scared in my life. I wondered if Mark had found out about us. Maybe the whole unreal employment offer and getting a brand-new Mercedes was a trap for me to sleep in their home so he could kill me in the middle of the night and then kill his wife too.

What if, in the middle of the night, Angelina got horny and came to my bed with her husband being in the next room?!

At that time, I had a strong feeling that Mark could have been the Mafia Boss in Las Vegas.

Angelina told me that Mark was also building high-rise buildings in other countries…Australia, Singapore, Macao, and the Middle East.

How could someone become so rich and so powerful in just ten years after starting from nothing? He must have had a connection with the Mafia.

On the surface, he was a very nice and friendly man, but underneath, he could be brutal. Only God knew how many of his competitors he had strangled with his own hands and probably buried in the desert around Las Vegas.

Angelina said he was a religious man and they went to church every Sunday. While he was in the church with his family, someone was probably carrying out his order of strangling his competitors, like in the Godfather movies.

I started to think Cristina had probably arranged everything and asked Angelina and Mark to strangle me in the middle of the night and get rid of me quietly.

Mark and Angelina could have been working together as a team. They had fooled me so cleverly by offering me that unreal employment opportunity and buying me a brand-new Mercedes convertible.

They wanted me to trust them and sleep in their home, so that in the middle of the night, Mark could get rid of me. I thought, *Tonight could be my last night alive, so I better fight.*

I couldn't escape from the window because the alarm would go off. But I unlocked it so that, if needed, I could open it quickly and escape.

I put a chair under the doorknob and put the couch in front of the chair, then I pushed my bed next to the couch so no one could push the door open.

I lay in bed with my clothes and shoes on, in case he tried to push the door open. That way, I could immediately open the window and run away.

I BEGGED MY SON TO SAVE ME

I texted my son, so if I vanished, he would know what happened to me.

Me: "Son, I am in big trouble. I need your help."

Son: "Dad, sure. Tell me how I can help you."

Me: "I am sleeping at the home of a family. The husband seems to be the Mafia boss in Las Vegas."

Son: "What?! Sleeping at the Mafia boss's home? How did that happen?"

Me: "They tricked me. His wife asked me to become her Secret Boyfriend and had an affair with me. She then invited me to their home, which is a mansion.

The husband offered me an unreal job of running his land-developing business. He then promised to buy me a brand-new white Mercedes convertible, first thing tomorrow morning.

"They fooled me and I accepted his offer and agreed to sleep in their guest room. I think tonight, while I am sleeping, he will come to strangle me. The whole thing looks sooo suspicious!"

Son: "Let me call the Las Vegas police department to come and help you."

Me: "No...Absolutely not! Do not call them. It will make the matter worse. I think he owns the whole Las Vegas police department by bribing them. This man is very powerful, clever, and very dangerous. Only the FBI can help me.

"I am going to send you his name, the address of his business, and the address of the house where I am staying tonight. If tomorrow morning, you cannot get ahold of me, it means that he strangled me, so immediately contact the FBI."

Son: "Dad, did you say you had an affair with the Mafia boss's wife?"

Me: "No, she had an affair with me."

Son: "Hahahaha…The wife of the Mafia boss in Las Vegas had an affair with you? Hahahaha. How do you know his wife?"

Me: "She is the younger sister of my wife, Cristina, who ran away. I believe Cristina asked her sister, Angelina, to kill me silently. Angelina got close to me, had an affair with me, and then invited me to their mansion, so that in the middle of the night, her husband, Mark, could strangle me and then bury my body in the desert outside Las Vegas. Because Mark is the perfect person to carry out this mission. He has probably done it in the past."

Son: "Hahahaha…The younger sister of Cristina is the wife of the Mafia boss in Las Vegas and had an affair with you? Hahahaha…OMG…that is so funny."

Son continued: "Dad, sorry to say that, but I think instead of calling the FBI, you should call 911 to take you to the hospital for a mental evaluation. Dad, your story is so bizarre that if you write a novel about it, you will sell millions of copies and will retire comfortably.

"Hahahaha…OMG…hahahaha…so, so, so funny. Dad, I didn't know that you had such a creative mind. Get on your laptop right now and start

writing your novel. The best title for it would be,
Secret Boyfriend.

"Hahahaha…Hahahaha…I cannot stop laughing…
Hahahaha…"

It was so sad that even my own son didn't believe
me. But I texted him Mark's name and the address
of the house anyway. I went online and searched
how to defend myself when someone was trying to
strangle me.

I could barely sleep that night, and when I did, I
kept one eye open. Luckily, nothing happened.
When I woke up, I re-arranged the furniture back to
how it was. I opened the door and went to the
kitchen.

Mark was preparing the coffee. I said, "I have to run
to my apartment to take care of something for my
son."

Mark was very friendly and gave me a cup of coffee.
I took it and said I would drink it in my car. I was
afraid that he might have put poison in it to kill me.
I went to my apartment, took a shower, and got
fresh.

Mark had a very unhealthy lifestyle. He was a hard
worker, heavy drinker, and fast-food junkie who did

not exercise. He had no fun at all. His only focus was money, money, and even more money. He was like a time bomb who could have a heart attack and die at any moment!!!

While Mark was treating me like his younger brother, I was the Secret Boyfriend to his wife. I was ashamed of myself, but only because it was better than feeling helpless in my apartment.

I was playing a very dangerous game, but I decided to go ALL IN both as a Secret Boyfriend to Angelina and as a loyal employee in Mark's business. I could not afford to lose either of them. I was hoping that I wouldn't get caught and get strangled.

So far, this is how I would have described the three of us:

Mark: A time bomb who could die at any moment.
Me: The Secret Boyfriend to Angelina, and a trusted employee to Mark.
Angelina: Hot, Hot, I mean, HOT!!!

Around eight a.m., Mark's office manager called me. She said, "Mr. Noor, Mark asked me to buy a brand-new white Mercedes convertible for you. I called the dealership, and they actually have a couple onsite. I made a ten a.m. appointment for you with the sales department to take care of you. Is ten a.m. good for you?"

"Yes, of course," I replied.

I was at the dealership thirty minutes before 10 a.m. and looked around. The sales agent showed me the cars that they had. WOW...It was beyond me. Going from my Honda Civic to a brand-new Mercedes convertible was a big jump. I signed the papers, and they gave me the key. I drove to Mark's office to thank him.

Even after picking up my Mercedes convertible, I still didn't know whether Mark was treating me like his younger brother or if he was training me to be the next Mafia boss in Las Vegas.

In either case, I accepted the car and the job offer because the money was very good, either legally or illegally. When I started working there, I kept my eyes open for any signs of illegal activities or any Mafia connections. I wanted to be careful so that I wouldn't get strangled.

Mark was a man of his word. He did what he had promised me. Now, it was my turn to do what I had promised him, and that was to take his land-development business to the moon. I had years of experience in construction and real estate, but not in real-estate development on a large scale.

Mark introduced me to his staff as a very close and dear family member and assigned me a nice corner office with windows on both walls. He also assigned me a personal secretary. What a change in just a few days, all thanks to his wife, Angelina…the true love of my life!

When I started working there, I realized that Mark was a lot bigger and more successful than I first thought he was. Wow…what a huge success in just ten years after starting from nothing.

I asked him, "How did you become so successful?"

He said, "My burning desire to get ahead, and then sharing my blessings with others."

What a great lesson, and what a great place to work and learn from him.

The first thing I did was call my ex-wife, Cristina. I said, "You have some mail that came to my post-office address. Let's meet at the parking lot of McDonald's on Las Vegas Blvd in front of the South Point Casino so you can pick it up."

She agreed, and of course, she came with her Secret Boyfriend in his twenty-year-old white Mercedes convertible with frosty front lights. It was absolutely no comparison to mine. She had come to brag about her Secret Boyfriend's car and to hurt me the most with my Honda Civic.

Cristina was shocked to see me with the latest model of the same white Mercedes convertible. She said, "Looks nice!!! What happened? When I was with you, you were flat broke. How did you get this car?"

I said, "Well…right after you left, I concluded a big real-estate deal with a big commission. I used part of my commission and paid cash to buy this car." Of course, she had no idea that her sister, her number one rival, had bought it for me.

I could see she was tempted to dump her boyfriend and jump into my brand-new car. She had no loyalty. She was never a loyal wife to me. Her only loyalty was to the man with the better Mercedes.

I gave her the mail, proudly said goodbye to her Secret Boyfriend, who felt like a loser seeing all my success in just a few days, and I drove away. I have never felt that good. I immediately texted Angelina about meeting her jealous sister. Angelina was delighted.

I went back to my office and started working. Mark became my mentor. He helped me like a caring older brother. At the same time, I'd never had anyone who loved me as much as his wife. She wanted to marry me for life.

Shortly after I started my work at Mark's office, Angelina called me and said, "Babe, I miss you sooo much, and I want to see you badly. Can we go somewhere, just the two of us with your sexy car?"

I said, "Sweetheart, I left your house this morning. How could you miss me so fast? I have to focus on my work; otherwise, Mark will fire me."

In a very romantic way, she said, "I am going to cook some delicious Filipino food for you. Can we eat together at your apartment this lunchtime? Please...Please...Pleeeeease..."

I said, "Babe, my apartment is a mess. After Cristina ran away, I was so depressed that I didn't clean it."

She said, "Don't worry, we can eat first and then while you are taking a nap and resting, I'll clean your apartment. Please...Please...Pleeeeease?"

I couldn't resist and said, "Okay, twelve fifteen p.m., my apartment, and this is the address." Wow...I felt like I had died and gone to heaven. My wife would never have done such a thing. These two sisters were different.

Mark walked into my office and said, "Paul, I am sooo glad you joined us. I can see a great future for you and for our company. It's good to have someone like you whom I can fully trust." He then said, "Let's go out to lunch and celebrate our new and exciting future."

I said, "Mark, I would love to, but I have to meet someone special. How about tonight for dinner?"

He said, "Sounds good, Paul. I'll tell my secretary to make a reservation at a nice restaurant with an overview of the city. I will ask Angelina to join us too. I am sure she would be delighted to be with you."

I silently said, *Yes...I am sure she will.*

I arrived early at my messy apartment to do some basic cleaning so Angelina would be able to at least walk through my place. It was a huge mess, like my apartment had been hit by an atomic bomb. Around noontime, I saw her drive in and park her sexy red Mercedes convertible next to mine.

My apartment complex was for medium- to low-income people. Half of the people in my complex were either taxi or Uber drivers, and my Honda Civic was a perfect fit.

Suddenly going from a Civic to my expensive new Mercedes, people would think I had become a drug dealer. Having two expensive Mercedes convertibles next to each other was even worse. Neighbors could get suspicious and call the Police SWAT team. I could imagine them raiding my apartment to see what was going on.

I left Angelina in the apartment and immediately went outside and moved both cars to the shopping center close to my complex. When I got back to my apartment, Angelina had changed her dress to a working uniform but still looked sexy and attractive.

She had already cleaned my breakfast table and put the food on it. She was waiting for me so we could eat together. She gave me a big hug and a juicy kiss.

She put only one plate on the table. I said, "Angelina, why only one plate? Don't you want to eat?"

She said, "No, we are going to eat from one plate." She put one spoonful of food in my mouth, then one in hers. WOW...every day was getting better and better. True Heaven on Earth!

After eating lunch, Angelina said, "Sweetie, why don't you go to your bedroom and rest? I'll start cleaning your apartment." About an hour and a half later, she knocked on my door and said, "Come and see if you like it." WOW...she had completely cleaned and re-arranged everything in such a short time. It was unbelievable.

She then said, "I'm going to take a shower now. Can I use your towel, babe?"

I said, "Of course," and she started taking off her clothes right in front of me. I left the bedroom to give her privacy.

A few minutes later, she called to me and said, "Babe...Babe...I don't know how to adjust the hot water." I was surprised because my hot- and cold-water knobs were very simple. How could she not be able to adjust them?

I went to the bathroom. She was in her panties and bra, at least not totally nude. In a very sexy voice, she said, "Can you adjust the water for me?" After I fixed it, she gave me a hug and kiss, and said, "You are my man! I can lean on you."

WOW!!! *You are my man! I can lean on you.* And that was just for adjusting the hot water. I felt so good.

My confidence went sky-high. Cristina had never said such a thing.

She then, in a sweet voice, said, "My love, why don't you take a shower with me so you can be fresh for work?" It was hard to resist. At least she had her panties and bra on.

She started undressing me and took my hands and pulled me into the shower. She hugged me and started kissing me, and then took off her bra and put it around my neck. She pulled me toward her very tightly and kissed me some more. O...M...G...Heaven on Earth! Sooo refreshing!!!

I said silently, *Cristina, thank you very much for running away.*

I returned to the office about mid-afternoon. Mark came to me and said, "How was your meeting with your special friend?"

I said, "Sooo refreshing!!!"

He then said, "My secretary made a reservation for the three of us for that restaurant I talked about earlier. I haven't told Angelina yet, but I am sure she will be delighted to spend some time with you. I am so proud of her for helping you to get out of that suicidal thinking. I want the two of you to stay close to each other."

I said, "We will do our best. You don't have to worry about that AT ALL!"

He then said, "Paul, I know a lovely Filipina lady who is divorced and looking for a nice man like you. Do you want me to invite her, so you can meet each other? I know that you like Filipina ladies."

I said, "No, no, no…absolutely not. I already found one, and she doesn't allow anyone to get close to me." I meant Angelina, of course.

He then said, "Why don't you invite her, so we can get to know her?"

I said, "I'll try."

In the evening, we met at a beautiful, high-class restaurant with an astonishing view of Las Vegas. Angelina wore a lovely and sexy dress. I couldn't take my eyes off her boobs.

Mark said, "Sweetheart, I've never seen you look this beautiful and sexy. I am sure it's because we have Paul back."

I told myself silently, *You got that one right!!!*

Mark asked me, "Paul, where is your Filipina lady you told me about? I thought you were going to bring her tonight?"

I said, "She is actually here with us now." Angelina's shock was evident. She was afraid I was going to tell Mark that I was her Secret Boyfriend. She could hardly breathe.

Mark laughed and looked around. He said, "Where is she? Angelina is the only lady here."

I said, "She is here, right at this table."

The blood drained from Angelina's face. Her heart almost stopped.

"She is here in my heart and will stay here for the rest of my life, forever," I continued.

Mark said, "What a sweet and loyal man you are, Paul. That lady must be very lucky to be part of your life.

"We are sooo lucky to have you as part of our family too. Ever since you joined us, Angelina has been a different person. It must be because of you! Thank you, Paul, for bringing this much joy and excitement to her life."

Angelina breathed again. Under the table, she stroked my foot in a slow and loving way.

Mark said, "How romantic and thoughtful. Paul is such a loyal man to his lady. I have a lot to learn from him. I want to be the same to you, Angelina." He looked at me and said, "Paul, I hated what your wife did to you, but on the bright side, you already found the love of your life."

Angelina and Cristina really hated each other and hadn't spoken in ten years. They had completely different personalities, but they had two amazingly similar desires.

They both liked Mercedes convertibles, and they both liked having a Secret Boyfriend, and were not afraid of that, even with their husbands being next to them.

So far, this is how I would have described the three of us:

Mark: A time bomb who could have a heart attack and die at any moment.
Me: In business, loyal to Mark, my "older brother," and Secret Boyfriend to his wife, the love of my life. I was ashamed of myself, and felt so low and dirty. I wanted to get out, but I didn't know how to escape.

Angelina: Hot…Hot…I mean, HOT, and wasn't going to let me go without a FIGHT. She wanted to use me to escape from her marriage and be with me.

THE HEART ATTACK

As we were eating and laughing, suddenly, Mark felt a sharp pain in his chest and fell to the floor. I screamed, "Help! Help! Call an ambulance quickly!"

Luckily, there was a nurse in the restaurant who came to help. She kept him alive until the ambulance came and took him to the hospital, which was close by.

Angelina and I followed the ambulance to the hospital. They immediately took him to the emergency room. After doing the preliminary exam, the doctor said, "It was a heart attack, and he needs surgery. He is alive, and I think we can save him."

The next morning, Mark was able to talk, and we told him what happened.

The doctor came and talked to him in front of us. She said, "According to your wife, you are a workaholic, an alcoholic, eating fast food a lot, and not doing any exercise. Your wife said you don't go on vacation regularly, and when you go, you work there too."

She then continued, "We have to do surgery. I am confident that we can save you, but if this happens again, you may never get another chance.

"You have to completely change your lifestyle. From this moment, you cannot be in touch with your company and their daily activities. Whether you like it or not, you must assign someone else to do it for you. No more tension and stress for you, at least not for now."

Mark looked at me and said, "Paul, the only person I fully trust is you. I want to give you the full power of attorney, to make decisions on my behalf, sign on my behalf, and run my organization on my behalf."

He then said, "Paul, I love you like my younger brother, and I know that Angelina loves you too. Would you do it for me...please?"

I said, "Mark, I love you like my older brother. I will accept it, but on one condition: you must listen to me. I want to make sure that, from this moment, your lifestyle will completely change. If I see that you are not doing that, as your trusted younger brother, I will get completely out of this deal."

Mark shook hands with me and said, "You got it, brother. Please save my company. I want to enjoy

Angelina and our ten-year-old son." We shook hands again and gave each other a bear hug.

He then called his attorney to prepare the papers for giving me the full power of attorney. The attorney prepared everything, and they were signed a couple of hours before Mark went for surgery.

Mark immediately called his vice president and the office manager to announce the decision.

He also recorded a short video from his hospital bed and sent it to all his employees. He made me a partner in his empire, too, and with a generous package.

What he said brought tears to my eyes. The way he trusted me and treated me like his younger brother, and only a few hours before, I took a shower with his wife. I felt so embarrassed and so ashamed of myself.

His heart attack was a wake-up call for him, and for me too. I hated being Angelina's Secret Boyfriend. I felt so low in life. It was a dirty job, and I had decided to get out of it, but Angelina really wasn't going to let me go without a fight. She wanted me to help her escape from her miserable marriage.

I immediately went back to work and introduced myself to the senior staff. They all welcomed and updated me on the daily activities.

The surgery went well, but Mark had to stay in the hospital for his recovery. When my life fell apart, Mark saved me. Now, as his trusted younger brother, it was my turn to save his life, his company, and most importantly, his marriage, and I was determined to do that.

A few days after the surgery, I had a private talk with Mark and Angelina. I said, "Mark, if you want to have your wife and son back, you have to stop drinking immediately, change your diet, exercise regularly, and take a vacation with them.

"You will not call your company. Everything has to go through me, and you will call me rarely." He agreed to do that and was excited to start a new life with them, but Angelina wasn't excited at all. She wanted to go on vacation with me.

I had decided to pretend to Angelina that I was still her Secret Boyfriend, the way that she wanted, but my intention was to completely get out of it. I wanted her to go back to Mark, my brother, I mean my real brother.

Angelina looked at Mark and said, "Honey, we are glad that the surgery went well. I am sure Paul is a capable man to handle our business.

"I was thinking, maybe every day after dropping our son off at school, I should go to the office for a few hours and help Paul, since I am more familiar with our business and also to give him some moral support."

I said silently, *Holy shit…NOOOOO!!! She is not giving up on me.*

Mark said, "Brilliant idea, sweetheart!!! That would be awesome. Yes, please do whatever you can to help and keep him happy and support him.

"Make sure to cook some delicious Filipino food and take it to him for lunch. Otherwise, like me, he will eat fast food and pizza at work."

Angelina said, "Of course, I will do that. And I will give him a shoulder massage during his lunchtime too."

Mark replied, "Honey, that would be a great idea. Paul has brought blessings to our lives, especially to you. Do whatever you think is necessary to keep the relationship between the two of you solid."

Angelina then said to Mark, "Honey, how about building a shower in his office, so he can take a shower at lunchtime?"

I screamed, "NOOOOO...No shower. Please, Angelina, you are too nice, but no shower. I can take a short nap at lunchtime and I will be fresh. Absolutely no shower." I knew what Angelina was thinking...to close my office door and take a shower with me.

I had to stop this shit. I had the major responsibilities of running Mark's development empire and saving his marriage. I didn't want to continue my relationship with Angelina.

We then left Mark's room. While walking through the hallway of the hospital, Angelina whispered into my ear and said, "Remember, I am half owner of the business. It means that you are working for me too." With a smile, she continued, "You better do what I ask you to do."

I then jokingly said, "Remember, I am running your organization now, and without me, your business cannot function. So, you better do what I ask you to do as well." We smiled at each other and headed toward the office.

When I became completely in charge of Mark's company, I hired a private investigator to see if any land developers had been strangled or had died in a suspicious way within the last ten years. None could be found.

I also hired a private accounting company to check out our financial activities in the last ten years. I wanted them to check for any illegal activities or any signs of bribery to the police chief in Las Vegas or any government officials. None could be found, except for Mark's generous contributions, but nothing illegal.

I then realized that Mark was an honorable man. He was a visionary and had become so successful because of, as he said, "my burning desire to get ahead and then sharing my blessings with others."

MEETING THE CHIEF OF POLICE

When I became the CEO of the company, one day, Police Chief Johnson called me and introduced himself. He said, "I have heard that you are now in charge of the company. I would like to meet with you and personally thank you for your company's past support and financial contributions to our police department. When would be the best time to meet with you?"

I said, "How about tomorrow at ten a.m.?" He agreed.

We met at 10 a.m. in my office. Regardless of his huge responsibility and position, he was a very humble man.

He thanked me for all of Mark's financial contributions to the police department, and for bringing peace and prosperity to the under-privileged communities. He commented, "Mark always believed in sharing his blessings with others. I hope you will continue his passion."

I said, "Chief, I promise I will do that, but first, you have to do me a big favor!"

Chief got curious and wanted to make sure I wouldn't ask anything illegal.

He asked suspiciously, "What's that?"

I said, "Could I take a picture with you like the one that Mark has?" I showed him the portrait of himself and Mark that was hung in our office.

Chief smiled and said, "You scared me...haha! That is an easy one. For sure..."

I immediately took a similar picture with him. I made a portrait with a nice frame. At the bottom, I wrote, "With my buddy, Chief Johnson."

I made two portraits. I hung one in our office at work, and one in the family room of my home—definitely not in the guest room.

I didn't want to scare the guests in my home into thinking that I could be the Mafia boss in Las Vegas and own the police department.

Chief Johnson and I became good buddies in serving the under-privileged communities in Las Vegas.

So far, this is how I would have described the three of us:

Mark: Started a fresh life with Lovely Angelina and their son.
Me: I decided to become a real gentleman and save my brother's marriage and business.
Angelina: Hot…Hot…I mean, HOT…and wasn't going to let me go without a FIGHT. She wanted to escape from her marriage and be with me.

Secret Boyfriend   —   Paul Noor

Chapter Three

The Bloody Wedding

After being the Secret Boyfriend to two Filipina sisters, it was finally time to choose my wife. These two sisters had not spoken to each other for ten years. They hated each other and had no idea that I was the Secret Boyfriend to both of them.

I told them that I would like to have a gathering of about two hundred family members and friends in Davao City, Philippines, where they were from, to announce who my wife would be. But I wanted both sisters to attend, even though it seemed impossible to have them under one roof.

I was surprised by how easily they both agreed to come. I think it was because each thought they would be the one I would select as my new wife, in front of the other sister.

I also told them that when they met, they had to be respectful to each other. I told them they would sit at the front table with their mom in between them. When I told their mom about it, she was delighted.

The celebration started at 6 p.m. I arranged live music, high-end food, and dancing—as high-class as it could get.

After the dinner, I took the microphone and went on the stage to announce my new bride. Everyone was excited to hear it, so they stopped playing the music, servers stopped serving food, and the room was quiet. You could have heard a pin drop from a distance.

I said, "Ladies and Gentlemen, tonight is a very special night. It's special because I see many friends and family members. It's special because we see these two beautiful sisters, who had a frosty relationship, now sitting on either side of their mother. It's special because we see this beautiful family united again.

"But tonight is particularly special because, for the first time, I will announce to my family members and friends who my new bride will be."

When I said that, I could see Cristina's and Angelina's faces beaming with JOY. They were both expecting I would announce their name as my new bride.

I stood up firmly, took a deep breath, and bravely said, "The best way to live is by being honest, and tonight, I want to be very honest. Tonight, for the first time, I want to announce that I was the Secret Boyfriend to these two beautiful sisters and I fell in love with both of them. Tonight, I will announce who my wife will be."

The two sisters and the audience were shocked; they could not believe it. A few people got angry and said, "That is horrible...Shame on you!!!" But one brave man stood up and said very loudly, "That's awesome!!! Can you teach me how to do it?"

I said, "Yes, of course, but wait, it gets even juicier."

You should have been in the room to see these two sisters. Both screamed in unison and said, "You son of a bitch, you were Secret Boyfriend to both of us?!" Yet, each was still hoping she would be the one I would pick.

I said, "I'll start with Angelina...Angelina, when I first met you at Manila Airport, although it was only for two hours, I fell deeply in love with you. Even though we never expressed our love for each other, it never died. And when my wife, Cristina, ran away with her Secret Boyfriend, you immediately jumped on the opportunity and asked me to become your Secret Boyfriend.

"At that time, I was so depressed, broken into pieces, I could not move on; I could not eat and didn't want to leave my messy apartment. Then... like an angel, you came into my life and lifted me up with your love.

"It was like you opened the door to heaven for me. You instantly showed me what true love is. Without you, I could never have gotten back on my feet. You saved me. You really DID! I will be eternally thankful to you."

At this time, Angelina couldn't have been happier. I could see the joy on her face. She was confident she was the one I would pick as my wife.

I looked at Cristina and said, "Sweetheart, you were the love of my life for twelve years. You stole my heart, from the first moment I met you. For twelve years, you were my baby, my other half, my princess.

"I also helped you become a US citizen so that you could get your US passport...and to become independent. But when you became independent, you ran away with your Secret Boyfriend, instead of paying me back with your love and support so that I could get back on my feet, too."

At this time, Angelina was super confident she would be the one I would pick.

I continued, "Cristina, you left me in a very heartless way. But recently, you came back to me and said how sorry you are for what you did. You asked for my forgiveness, but I wasn't ready to forgive you. You thanked me profusely for all I have done for you, but I wasn't ready to even listen to you.

"Since your relationship with your boyfriend wasn't going well, you asked me to become your Secret Boyfriend. Maybe you asked me because of my brand-new Mercedes convertible.

"You tried your hardest to show me the better side of you, which I had never seen before. You wanted me to become your Secret Boyfriend, but I was already the Secret Boyfriend to your sister, Angelina, and she immediately showed me the door to heaven and pure love at the time I needed it the most. I didn't need any more love. I was very happy with Angelina, and she was very happy being with me, too."

At this time, Angelina knew that she was the clear winner. I looked at her with a smile and said, "My dear Angelina, my real love, you saved me with your love at a time when I was so desperate. You immediately asked me to be your Secret Boyfriend, and that was the best thing that happened to me.

"Your husband, Mark, treated me like his younger brother and even made me a partner in his organization. When Mark had a heart attack, I decided to pay him back by being his caring brother, by saving his business, and most importantly, by saving his marriage.

"I wanted you and Mark to get back together. I wanted to be a good friend to both of you. I didn't want to be your Secret Boyfriend anymore...just a best friend to both of you."

Everyone in the room was wondering which direction I was going and which sister I would marry. I continued, "Angelina, you were the true love of my life. You stole my heart when I first met you at Manila Airport. It was so wonderful to be your Secret Boyfriend.

"In front of everyone here tonight, I say I love you sooo much, but I cannot marry my brother's wife. Mark is my brother...actually, he is better than my brother.

"Angelina, I love you sooo much, but now, I love you only as a BEST friend, and for life. You are a true angel, and I would like to stay close to you and your husband. I am glad I am a business partner with you and your husband and will get to see you more often."

In front of everyone, I gave her a bouquet of roses and hugged her. It was emotional and the longest hug I have ever given to anyone. Just like that, I went from being her Secret Boyfriend to being her BEST friend.

The audience gave us a standing ovation, and some were crying with tears of joy. We gave each other a kiss on the cheek, and she sat down, feeling emotional.

At this time, Cristina did not believe what she had heard. If I was not marrying Angelina, it must have meant I would marry her. She was full of joy and could not control her excitement.

The whole audience could not believe I was going to marry my ex-wife. They were confused and eager to know my final decision.

I looked at Cristina and said, "Sweetheart, you were my baby for twelve years. You were the love of my life. You were my other half. But as soon as I helped you to get your education and US passport, you ran away from me, instead of paying me back with your love and support, so I could get back on my feet as well.

"But you came back. You apologized, you asked for forgiveness, and I finally forgave you. You asked me to become your Secret Boyfriend, and I did. Even though we did not sleep together, and our relationship was like two good friends holding hands, walking, and talking, this time, I enjoyed you tremendously.

"So, I have decided not to marry you either. Just to be your BEST friend for life. I want to give you this bouquet of twelve red roses, one for each of those wonderful twelve years of being together.

"I want to be BEST friends with you two lovely sisters who are finally friends and united with your mother. Yes, I am not going to marry either of you."

The audience was shocked because I had thrown that luxury party to announce which sister would be my wife. If I was not going to marry either of the two sisters, then whom would I marry?

SECRET BOYFRIEND TO A THIRD LADY

I waited a few seconds while the audience members talked to each other, until they became completely quiet. Then I said, "Ladies and Gentlemen, the lady I will be marrying is here tonight, in this room."

Everyone looked at each other and started talking, wondering who that lady was. What was going on?!

I waited a few more seconds and then took a deep breath and bravely said, "Ladies and Gentlemen, as I said earlier, the best way to live is by being honest, and tonight, I want to be very honest. Tonight, I want to confess something. In addition to these two lovely sisters, I have also been the Secret Boyfriend to a third lady."

Suddenly, the mother of Cristina and Angelina, who until that time had been sitting quietly, exploded. She stood up, and with a loud voice, she said, "You son of a bitch...you were the Secret Boyfriend to three ladies, and you talk about being honest in life?! Shame on you!" She then asked, "Did you sleep with her?"

I said, "My honest answer is NO, absolutely NOT. She didn't even let me hold her hand, and there was no kissing at all." She moved back and all three of them were relieved that I hadn't slept with her.

The audience was shocked by the kind of lousy and useless Secret Boyfriend I was! No holding hands and no kissing?! What a loser!!!

I continued, "My third lady, whom I would like to marry, is here tonight. She is among us in this room." The audience suddenly erupted into motion and kept looking around; Some looked at their wives suspiciously, praying theirs wouldn't be the one going on the stage.

I then said, "Ladies and Gentlemen, it's time to introduce my future bride." With a joyful voice, I said, "My sweetheart, my baby, my future wife, would you please come on the stage and stand next to me?"

With my high position and income in the land-development business, everybody was looking for a sexy, elegant woman with expensive clothing and a purse to enter the stage.

But there was no lady except for a server with two glasses of champagne who had moved onto the stage and stood about ten feet from me on my left. She was waiting to serve drinks to me and my new bride.

The audience waited. There was no elegant lady entering the stage. I waited for a couple of minutes, until there was complete silence. The audience was puzzled; they had no idea what was going on.

Standing firmly, and with a smile full of joy, I said, "As we say in America, third time is the charm. My future bride, my princess, the love of my life, please come and stand next to me. Please give a big round of applause for my new bride."

The audience started clapping with enthusiasm and looked around the room. But there was no sign of a high-class, elegant lady with a stylish dress to walk on the stage.

At this time, the server who was on the stage got closer and stood next to me on my left and waited to serve drinks to me and my future bride. The audience got frustrated that there was no bride on the stage.

With an excited voice, I said, "It's my honor and privilege to introduce to you my future bride." I proudly looked at the server next to me and said, "Her name is Ann Ruby. She is the love of my life. She will be my new bride."

The audience erupted in disbelief. The confusion was getting worse and worse. They thought I was joking and fooling around with them. Marrying a hotel server!!! I could feel some of them were even angry and ready to leave the ballroom. They thought I was insulting them.

I continued, "Yes, you heard me right. I am going to marry this lovely lady. Her name is Ann Ruby. Well, let me correct that, her name is Dr. Ann Ruby...yes, Dr. Ann Ruby.

"She came from a poor family in a province of the Philippines. To support her family, she got a job as a server here in this hotel. Now, she is a successful doctor who specializes in stroke patients and works in a prestigious hospital in Las Vegas. She is the true love of my life."

In front of the audience, I pulled out the engagement ring and bent on my knee. While she still had her tray with two glasses of champagne on it, I said, "Dr. Ann Ruby, you are the true love of my life. Will you marry me?"

The audience erupted in joy and gave us a standing ovation. Dr. Ann Ruby screamed and said, "Yes...of course...of course...I love you, babe."

She gave me her left hand while she still had the tray and the two drinks on it in her right hand. I put the engagement ring on her finger and gave her a BIG kiss. The audience kept clapping and liked how my search for marriage had ended with Dr. Ann Ruby, a girl from a poor family, now getting engaged in this prestigious ballroom of the Marco Polo Hotel in Davao City, where she had once been a server.

We took those two glasses of champagne and celebrated. The whole event was beyond joyful. I said, "Sweetheart, I bought some clothes for you, they are in the room in the back. Why don't you go there with your lovely fellow servers, change your clothes, and then come back?"

About twenty of the servers in the hotel, while carrying the trays in their hands, escorted her to the back room. The audience had no idea what kind of dress I had bought for her.

HISTORY OF DR. ANN RUBY

Ladies and Gentlemen, while she is changing her clothes in the back room, let me talk very briefly about Dr. Ann Ruby. Before I met Cristina, I met Ann Ruby, and I instantly fell in love with her and knew I should marry her. I dated her for one week while I was in the Philippines, before going back to the United States.

Unfortunately, at that time, we had some challenges and couldn't work out our differences, but we stayed in touch for a couple of months. Then we broke up, but she was always in my mind and heart. I was hoping, one day, I would find her.

While my marriage with Cristina was falling apart, I tried to find her to see how she was doing. I was amazed to find out she was living in Las Vegas too. She was delighted I found her and asked her to go out for coffee. She gladly accepted.

The next day, we met at the coffee shop of the hospital where she was working. She came in wearing her white doctor's uniform with the name "Dr. Ann Ruby" on it. I almost cried when I saw her. She was as beautiful as she had been more than twelve years before, when she was my girlfriend.

We gave each other a hug and sat down. The attraction was again instant, at least from my side. We hadn't seen each other for more than twelve years, so we had lots of catching up to do.

When I first met her, she was the server in this hotel. She had something very special, and I immediately fell in love with her, and now, she is Dr. Ann Ruby, specializing in stroke patients.

I said, "Ann, tell me about it. How did you get here?"

She said, "Paul, after that painful breakup between us, I found an American man. Like you, he was a very caring, loving, sweet person. He was looking for a Filipina wife and I was looking for a husband. We were attracted to each other. We eventually got married and moved to the United States.

"He knew I was from a poor family and could not continue my education. He helped me go to college. Since I did well, he encouraged me to go to medical school, and I did. He supported me financially and morally. We have two children together. He actually took care of them so I could focus on my education.

"He told me, 'I want you to graduate from medical school, then go to the Philippines, wear your medical uniform with the name tag of Dr. Ann Ruby, and go to your province so your family can see you and be proud of you.'

"I asked him why he was so nice to me. He said, 'Because you brought the heavenly Filipina smile, love, and loyalty into my life, which I have never experienced before. Now, I want to pay you back by making you the princess of my life, your family, and the people in your province.'"

Then Dr. Ann Ruby burst into tears and said, "Paul, my husband is dying now. He has terminal cancer and he may die in a couple of months."

While crying, she continued, "My American husband, who helped me go from being a server in that hotel to a doctor, will not be able to enjoy the fruits of his unconditional love and support. Now, it's my goal to pay him back and to take care of him with love to the last minute of his life. I want to show him the Filipina love and loyalty, to the last minute."

What an angel…what an angel!!! I offered her my unconditional support and help. I said, "Dr. Ann Ruby, please let me know if there is anything I can do for you. I mean, anything. Please consider me as your BEST friend. Would you, please?" and she agreed.

She said, "Paul, I have to go back to work. I am so glad we found each other. We'll be in touch." We gave each other a friendly hug and she left, and I went back to my miserable life of living with Cristina—the marriage that was falling apart like a terminal cancer, too.

I went out with Dr. Ann Ruby a few times. One time, we walked in the park near the hospital where she was working. But it wasn't like before when we were boyfriend and girlfriend.

I could feel we both had feelings for each other, but she was keeping a distance while we were walking. A few times, I tried to slowly touch her hand and hoped to hold it, but she immediately pulled it back and wanted to keep the distance.

She then said, "Paul, we were the most loyal and romantic boyfriend and girlfriend, and I enjoyed every second of those moments. I feel there is still an attraction between us. But now, my loyalty is one hundred percent only for my husband, who is dying.

"I cannot touch or hold your hand. I one hundred percent belong to my husband. I mean, one hundred percent. But I'd love for us to be best friends, especially in this time of turbulence in both of our lives."

Wow!!! What a great lady! What a loyal lady! I wish I would have married her when I had the chance. This is the Filipina lady I want to have in my life.

At that moment, I was confident I wanted to marry Dr. Ann Ruby. And I knew the condition would be to not touch her hand or hug her anymore—maybe just a light hug.

I decided to be Dr. Ann Ruby's BEST friend, as she requested. She was very busy as a doctor, but she cut her hours at work so she could personally take care of her dying husband. She refused to hire a caregiver to do it. She wanted to kiss and hug him in those final days of his life.

I was so impressed by her Filipina loyalty and dedication…a true Filipina who stayed to pay her husband back with her love and support.

A few times, I picked up their two children from school and brought food for them. Dr. Ann Ruby said, "Paul, as much as I really appreciate your unconditional support and help, I'd prefer not to introduce you to my husband.

"He is dying now, and I don't want him to get suspicious about you being my Secret Boyfriend. I want him to die in peace." What she said brought tears to my eyes and I gladly agreed to that.

A few weeks later, her husband died at home with Dr. Ann Ruby by his side. It was a peaceful departure from this physical world. I helped Dr. Ann Ruby with the funeral. It was emotional and very respectful.

I tried not to get too close to her. I didn't want her friends and coworkers to get suspicious about me being her Secret Boyfriend because she had clearly told me she only wanted me to be her BEST friend.

During the funeral, Dr. Ann Ruby gave a touching speech. She said, "I came from a poor family in the Philippines, but my beloved American husband saw something special in me. He saw the diamond in the rough.

"He worked tirelessly on me with his support, dedication, and unconditional love until I became a doctor and received my specialty in stroke patients. It was his dream that, one day, we would go back to my province in the Philippines, and I would wear my white doctor's uniform, with the name tag of Dr. Ann Ruby on it, and with the stethoscope around my neck.

"With that uniform, he wanted me to meet my family members and their children, and the poor people in our province. He didn't want me to brag about it; instead, he wanted me to inspire those children that even a poor child from that province can be a doctor in a prestigious hospital in America.

"It hurts me a lot that his dream did not get fulfilled. But, sweetheart, I promise to you I will do it and I will do my best to inspire the people in my province." She burst out crying and sat down.

At that moment, I promised myself I would do my best to steal Dr. Ann Ruby's heart, to marry her, and we would go to her province while she was wearing her hospital uniform. But I didn't know when she would be ready for a new life.

I stayed in close contact with her, and a few days later, I invited her for coffee again, and she gladly accepted. I didn't want anyone else to steal her heart. I wanted Dr. Ann Ruby. I wanted her to be my wife for life.

I knew what my limit was, and I didn't want to cross the line. I was waiting until she was ready to make the move. The coffee date went well, and then she asked me to go for a walk in the same park near the hospital.

Inviting me to walk in the park?! Was that a good sign? Was she trying to tell me something? Was she ready for me?

It was a beautiful day. We started walking, and again, I tried to keep my distance from her and not touch her hands. I loved her so much and I didn't want to risk losing her. I wanted her to be mine...
FOREVER.

As we were walking, she said, "Paul, you were my boyfriend, and I felt I could not separate from you. I still have feelings for you. But I still want to be loyal to my husband and be respectful and thankful to him for all the things he has done for me.

"I don't want to do anything for at least one year— absolutely nothing, no touching, no holding hands, and absolutely no kissing.

"If you agree to that, I still want to see you regularly because I feel good when I am with you. You are a healer, especially in this time of my family crisis. What do you think?"

I definitely didn't want to risk losing her. I wanted to be with her to the last day of my life. I immediately said, "Absolutely, YES. Let's be each other's BEST friend."

She wanted us to have a heart-to-heart relationship, and I agreed to that. It was a great walk in that romantic park. It was pure love between us.

Our relationship continued like that for a year, until the anniversary of the passing of her husband. She asked me if I could go with her to his grave and pray together, and of course, I gladly accepted.

We went to his grave and she started praying and thanking him for all he had done for her. She said, "Honey, we had a wonderful time together, and I cherished every moment of that. I guarantee you that, one day, I will meet you in heaven.

"Because you love me sooo much, I am sure you want me to move on, and I want to move on too. By doing that, I will be a better mother for our two children and a better doctor in the hospital. Those are the two things that were very important to you as well."

She then said something that completely surprised me. She said, "Honey, I am sure you want me to move on. I have a friend here with me who is a very nice man. He helped me a lot as a friend. Just like you, he cares for me and for our children a lot.

"Today, on the one-year anniversary of you going to heaven, I want to get your permission so I can start dating him and to get to know him. Both of us want to have your blessing." She then said a prayer and we left.

Wow!!! What a surprise. My love was ready for me, but I was still afraid to touch her hand. As we were walking toward my car, for the first time, she slowly touched and held my hand. It was the first time in more than thirteen years, from when we were boyfriend and girlfriend. It was the sweetest walk in a cemetery.

After we sat in the car, she gave me a big hug and a kiss and said, "I love you, babe...I love you, babe. Thank you for coming back." We were deeply in love again. I was determined to treat Dr. Ann Ruby like a princess, even though she already was a princess.

THE BRIDE IS COMING OUT

Finally, Dr. Ann Ruby was ready to come out of that back room. At this time, the music started to play, and in front of the shocked audience, Dr. Ann Ruby came out of the back room in a beautiful wedding dress. She looked like a princess.

The twenty servers with the trays in their hands escorted her to the front. It was a surprising moment for the audience. One surprise after another, but they seemed to enjoy it, because it was getting better and better. It was a wedding they would probably never forget.

Dr. Ann Ruby gracefully approached the stage and I moved forward, held her hand, and helped her to come on the stage. I had arranged for someone to officiate the wedding. In one night, I went from being a dirty Secret Boyfriend to the proud husband of a true angel, Dr. Ann Ruby.

I could see Angelina was very happy, but I was not sure about Cristina. I had tried to end my relationships with them respectfully. And I was determined to be the BEST friend to both.

I was confident I had the blessing of Angelina, but I wasn't sure about Cristina. She had been hoping to come back to me and re-marry. On the surface, she was pretending she was happy, but I could feel the anger behind her facade.

I had secretly invited four of Dr. Ann Ruby's friends from Las Vegas to attend the wedding—two Filipina doctors, one Hispanic, and one a white American. One of them was an emergency room doctor, one specialized in stroke patients, and the other two were regular doctors.

At this time, I invited them to come to the front of the ballroom. When Dr. Ann Ruby saw them, she burst into tears of joy, hugged them tightly, and could not believe they had come. She also hugged me for arranging that secret trip.

Those four ladies had been sitting in the back, watching the whole event unfold. It was shocking to them as well. When it was time for them to come forward, they put on their white doctors' uniforms with stethoscopes around their necks.

After the wedding was done, the live music started and special dancing with choreography like a Disney movie, like *Beauty and the Beast*, was performed. Twenty servers of the hotel were part of the dancing too.

It was an unforgettable night, and everyone seemed to enjoy it, except Cristina. I even danced with Angelina and Cristina separately, so that I could end my relationships with them with respect.

GUN SHOT

At the end of the wedding, Dr. Ann Ruby and I said goodbye and headed for our honeymoon. We went outside of the hotel and sat in my white Mercedes convertible, which had been decorated for the groom and bride, while Angelina, Cristina, and a few friends came outside to wish us well.

We left, and the guests went to the ballroom to continue dancing and celebrating. And, of course, we turned off our cell phones to make sure we wouldn't be interrupted. We just wanted to enjoy each other.

After we left, Cristina could not handle the jealousy. She went to her room on the eleventh floor of the same hotel, extremely nervous and angry. She opened the safe box, took her handgun out, stood in front of the mirror, and with an angry voice, said, "I am going to make your wedding a bloody one, and that's my wedding gift to you! Tomorrow, you will be all over the news: A successful land developer had a bloody wedding. **ENJOY MY GIFT!!!**"

She put the handgun in her purse and went downstairs to the ballroom, where the celebration was ongoing, and people were still dancing and enjoying that unforgettable night.

She pulled out the handgun and shot a couple of bullets into the ceiling to get everyone's attention. Then she put the handgun in her mouth to commit suicide.

Everyone screamed, "Don't do it…don't do it… please…don't do it!" Finally, she shot one bullet and fell in a pool of blood.

Her mom, sisters, and other family members rushed to her side, crying and screaming for help, but Cristina was not responding.

Dr. Ann Ruby's doctor friends who had come from Las Vegas rushed to help Cristina. The lead doctor was also a Filipina, an emergency doctor. Her name was Fedelyn, a very sharp and intelligent doctor who seemed capable.

She pushed everyone out and asked for space. They immediately started the work. The hotel shift manager called for an ambulance.

The other three doctors were helping Dr. Fedelyn save Cristina. Luckily, they verified she had a pulse and was breathing.

They did all the preliminary work, and the ambulance showed up quickly. They put Cristina in the back of the ambulance, and Dr. Fedelyn jumped in so she could be with Cristina.

The work started immediately. After a while, the doctor came out to the waiting room and told her mom, sisters, and a few family members, "I have good news and bad news. Cristina survived, but she lost her ability to walk and most of her speaking skills."

When we came back from our honeymoon, I heard about this horrible news. Dr. Ann Ruby and I rushed to the hospital. We saw Cristina on the bed...hopeless. I sat on her bed and asked her, "Where is your boyfriend?"

She could barely talk but said, "After my suicide attempt, he dumped me."

She was complaining that her right arm was numb. I immediately took her arm and started massaging it from top to bottom. She burst out crying and hugged me.

Then the doctor came to check on her. She said, "There is a slight chance she might regain her ability to walk and talk. But it can only be accomplished by her sheer determination, relentless therapy and practice, and with the help of a super-dedicated husband, boyfriend, or a very loyal and committed BEST friend." She then left.

I held Cristina's hand and said, "Remember, after our separation, I told you I wanted to be your BEST friend, but you never replied? Now, I want to ask you one more time: Cristina, I want to be your BEST friend…Will you accept my offer?"

She burst into tears again and could hardly talk. She said, "Paul, you are an angel. With all I have done to you, while I cannot walk and can barely talk, while I made your wedding a bloody one, while my boyfriend dumped me, while I am helpless in this hospital bed, while I have no one in America to help me, you offer me this?! How could I not see that side of you?!"

She then added, "That suicide attempt completely changed my life because, from today, I want to be an angel like you. I want to become an emergency room nurse to save people's lives. Paul, thanks for being my BEST friend. Will you stay with me until I graduate?"

I hugged her and said, "YES, I will be your BEST friend, all the way to the end."

Shortly after, we packed up our stuff and headed back toward Las Vegas, USA, with my lovely bride, Dr. Ann Ruby, on one side, and my disabled but determined ex-wife in the wheelchair.

As her new and committed BEST friend, I was determined to push her wheelchair all the way to a full recovery. Here, my new love story with Cristina started…a totally different love story…with the lady who could not walk and could barely talk.

At that moment, I felt my love for Cristina had never died.

Secret Boyfriend — Paul Noor

Chapter Four

I Fell in Love with My Ex-Wife, Cristina

When we arrived in Las Vegas, Cristina didn't have a place to live. As her new best friend and caregiver, I had to find a place specially designed for disabled people like her, which would take a few days. I asked my lovely wife, Dr. Ann Ruby, if Cristina could temporarily stay with us. Of course, she gladly accepted. So, from the airport, we went directly to our home.

Before going on our trip, I hired someone to decorate my home for my new bride, Dr. Ann Ruby. I didn't tell her about it, as I wanted it to be a surprise. And now, I had to take my disabled ex-wife with us, too, and let her sleep in the next room. It was a very uncomfortable and awkward situation, but I had no choice. I didn't want to rent a hotel room and leave Cristina there by herself. She couldn't have survived alone.

I slept on the couch in the family room, Dr. Ann Ruby stayed in our master bedroom, and Cristina stayed in our guest room. I left both the doors open. I didn't want Cristina to get hurt thinking that Dr. Ann Ruby and I were sleeping next to each other with the door being closed.

In the middle of the night, Cristina called me. She wanted to go to the bathroom. Since she could not walk or get herself out of the bed, I helped her and stayed with her until she was done. I then took her back to her room and put her to sleep like a good friend.

I woke up early in the morning and prepared breakfast. Dr. Ann Ruby had to go to work. I called Angelina to see if she could come and help me find a special facility for Cristina, and she managed to find a good one.

Angelina came to our home and the three of us went directly to that facility. It was a very nice place. Luckily, they had a room available for her. We immediately enrolled her, and I told the facility I would be the person responsible for Cristina.

I asked them to contact me anytime they needed me, twenty-four seven.

The next day, the therapy started—physical therapy for her walking and speech therapy for her talking. I told the facility I wanted to be there during the therapy for moral support, and to learn so I could help her by myself too.

Because of my personal past experience with severe stuttering, I knew how to help her with the speech therapy. Even though it was a different speech impediment, it was kind of similar. But I had no experience in helping her with walking, so I had to learn from the therapist.

I remember, after the gunshot, the surgeon in the hospital in Davao City, Philippines, told us, "There is a slight chance she might regain her ability to walk and talk. But it can only be accomplished by her sheer determination, relentless therapy and practice, and with the help of a super-dedicated husband, boyfriend, or a very loyal and committed BEST friend."

She said, "There is no damage to the walking and speaking parts of the brain. It's more like getting her confidence back."

Wow…it was like getting her confidence back! After being in business for so many years, falling and getting back on my feet so many times, and getting my confidence back, I had become an expert on that. I had to come up with a creative and out-of-the-box plan to help her.

When we went back to Las Vegas, I took her to a specialist to confirm what the doctor in Davao City had told us. After all the necessary tests, the doctor in Las Vegas came to the same conclusion. It was a matter of her sheer determination, relentless therapy, practice, and the support of a loyal and committed best friend. At that time, I knew there was a good chance I could help her.

Even though I was very busy at Mark's office, I still tried to attend the therapy sessions. I wanted to learn and educate myself so I could help her privately. Of course, Angelina and Mark didn't mind me taking off from work to help Cristina, who desperately needed my help and support. And my lovely Dr. Ann Ruby didn't mind it either.

Although my breakup with Cristina had happened in a painful way, I no longer felt anger toward her. That suicide attempt completely changed her life. When I decided to become her only caregiver, she became loving and was very thankful for every little thing I was doing for her.

While we were married, she hadn't been a thankful person at all. It's hard to help someone and not get any reward for your kindness. When you have a relationship like that, year after year after year, it will wear you down. You need to be appreciated so you can rejuvenate yourself and get new energy for moving forward.

It seemed like the bullet had gone through her mouth and turned on the "heavenly switch," making her tongue a thankful one. She was thanking me for every little thing I was doing for her, which was encouraging me to do more. She became very lovely and sweet. She became a TRUE ANGEL!!!

One time, Cristina asked me, "Why are you so nice to me? I harmed you so much, and I made your wedding a bloody one."

I said, "When we got married, I was in a very bad situation. It was in 2009, right after the collapse of the housing market. It had crushed my home-building business. I was down financially and emotionally.

"You helped me with your love and support until I got back on my feet. Now that you have fallen, I feel that I am obligated to help you get back on your feet too. I want to pay you back with love and support. I am not going to give up until you are fully back on your feet."

She said, "Paul, I am a disabled person now. I may never be able to walk again or speak properly. You are making a big commitment for something that may never happen. Are you going to stay with me forever?"

I said, "If needed, forever, but I am confident it will be sooner...a lot sooner."

I continued, "But first, you have to accept one hundred percent responsibility for your disability. It's your problem, not mine. If you blame it on others, you will be a victim and will never improve because victims never win."

I reminded her of what the surgeon in Davao City, Philippines, and the specialist in Las Vegas, had said: "There is no damage to the walking and speaking parts of the brain. It's more like you lost your confidence."

I said, "I am committed to helping you as your new best friend, but you have to show me your sheer determination to achieve it. It's teamwork. We both need each other."

I attended every therapy session with her. After therapy, I took Cristina to her room in that special healthcare facility. I had my laptop with me and did my work in her room, as I didn't want her to feel alone.

Sometimes, she needed to go to the toilet. Instead of calling for the staff to come and help her, I would do it myself…take her to the toilet, and then clean her and put her back in her bed.

I also helped her take baths. Take off her clothes, take her to the shower, help her wash her body, dry her, put on her panties, bra, and clothes, and take her back to bed again.

In all those years we were married, I had been in charge of putting her panties and bra on. I'd wanted to have the most loving and romantic relationship with her, and we had that. It had been so painful when, suddenly, everything fell apart.

I tried to control myself and be loyal to Dr. Ann Ruby, but my love for Cristina was getting out of control. I thought, *What if Dr. Ann Ruby finds out I am giving her baths, cleaning her body, and putting on her panties and bra? That would be the end of my marriage with her.*

One time while I was helping Cristina take a bath, Dr. Ann Ruby called her room to check on her. The cleaning lady picked up the phone and said, "They are in the shower. There is a man here who seems to be her ex-husband. The other day, he gave her a bath, dried her body, then put on her panties, bra, and clothes. Then he took her outside so she could get some fresh air. What a nice man. I wish I had an ex-husband like him. He is so sweet."

Dr. Ann Ruby then asked, "Do you know the name of that man?"

The cleaning lady said, "Yes, Paul Noor."

Dr. Ann Ruby screamed and said, "OMG…" and collapsed.

When Cristina and I got out of the shower, I asked the cleaning lady, "Did anyone call?"

She said, "Yes, Dr. Ann Ruby called to check on Cristina. I told her you are such a wonderful and romantic ex-husband. You are taking showers together, then drying her body and even putting on her panties and bra. So romantic!!!"

The cleaning lady then asked, "Who is Dr. Ann Ruby?"

I said, "OMG...she is my wife!"

The cleaning lady screamed and said, "OMG..." and collapsed.

Cristina and I both screamed and said, "OMG..." and we both collapsed...one on the bed and the other on the floor.

Someone brought food for Cristina. When she saw all three of us collapsed and unconscious on the bed and floor, she ran to the door and screamed, "OMG..." then also collapsed outside the door. The food and soup fell on the floor and spread all over the place. Other employees noticed it and called security.

When I got back on my feet, I knew I was in trouble with Dr. Ann Ruby. When I went home, she didn't mention anything. It was like nothing had happened. It seemed like the calm before the storm...I knew something would explode soon.

I continued my therapy with Cristina. I was taking her to physical and speech therapy regularly. I attended both and learned a lot too.

The therapy went on for a couple of weeks, but there weren't many improvements. She was still relying on me. So, I made a new plan for her, a totally out-of-the-box plan. I wanted to give her a shock so she would wake up and use all the hidden energy inside of her for walking.

I said, "Cristina, you know there is no damage to your walking and speaking skills. Doctors in both Davao City and Las Vegas confirmed that. It's time for you to walk; otherwise, you are wasting time— my time and your time.

"You should start walking now. I think you are relying on me. You must accept one hundred percent responsibility that this is your problem and not mine. I love to help you walk, but I don't want you to use me as your crutch all the time. I am a busy man. If you don't walk now on your own, I will leave you. I mean, right now."

She got so mad at me and said, "You are crazy! I am a disabled person, and you talk to me like that?! What you said was a slap in the face...it was insulting. You said you are doing this because you believe forgiveness is the key to ultimate happiness. You said you want to pay me back for helping you get back on your feet when we got married.

"You are a liar. You have one intention and that is to get revenge. Now that I am disabled and cannot walk and can barely talk, you think it's the best time to get revenge on a defenseless person like me."

She continued, "You are such a controlling and nasty person. You talk to me like I am your plumber in your construction business. You can't even talk to a plumber like that. Some of them make more money than you do. Have you hired a plumber lately? You talk to me like a piece of dirt."

She then said, "You know something, I might be disabled, but I have pride. I don't need your help, your fake kindness, or these crutches anymore. I want you to get lost…right now…get lost, right now…go, now!"

She threw her crutches toward me and started walking away like a baby who was taking her first step. It was slow, one step at a time, and it seemed as if she were using all her physical and mental energy to walk and tell me to get lost…

I screamed and followed her, "You are walking… you are walking! It worked…it worked! I am a genius. My plan worked! Yes, yes, yes! I am a genius. I am a genius."

She screamed back at me and said, "Get lost…I crushed your ego. You are a controlling person. You enjoy when others need you. I don't need you anymore. I will walk on my own. Get lost! Get lost!"

I screamed back at her and said, "You don't understand! It's a miracle…you are walking on your own. This is a miracle."

She finally realized she was walking without crutches. She couldn't believe it and got so scared that she fell on a bench nearby. I ran up to her and she hugged me. We were both celebrating. I was delighted to see her taking her first steps.

After resting for a few minutes, we decided to walk again. She couldn't do it. She needed special energy like last time. I said, "Let's repeat what you said a few minutes ago and do it with the same intensity."

She started repeating the same thing, but this time, it didn't work. I said, "This time, you were too nice. It doesn't work that way. You have to say it with anger. Release all your hidden energy and power. Also, this time, you missed the plumber part. That was your winning card." We both laughed, and she tried again and released lots of her hidden energy.

This time, she included the plumber part. It helped her some, but not much, so I had to lift her. She got on her feet and knowing that she could walk without crutches, she started walking again while I carried her crutches. I was walking next to her as a support, in case she needed me.

People were watching us in surprise. While she was struggling with her walking, I was carrying her crutches. It was a major accomplishment for the first day. She had broken the barrier. It was all in her mind. It was a matter of more practice. I could see her running soon. Since she'd just started, she couldn't walk for too long.

It was springtime, and a group of performers was singing a beautiful song in the park. People were gathered around them, enjoying the performance. The benches were all taken, but a couple saw Cristina struggling with walking, so they got up and let us sit.

The group was performing the song well, and while they were singing that lovely song, I got excited, and my love for Cristina re-ignited. I bought a flower from the nearby flower lady, and I gave it to Cristina and started dancing around her.

I could see the joy on her face at seeing me being in love with her. In the middle of the song, I kept one crutch facing horizontally. She grabbed it and lifted herself up. We continued dancing on either side of the crutch, while she was still holding the flower that I had given her.

The people around us were really enjoying our dance. At the end of the song, Cristina got closer to me and wanted to kiss me. I looked at the wedding band on my finger and didn't want to kiss her. Even though there was a great temptation. I was very loyal to my lovely wife, Dr. Ann Ruby.

Cristina put her hand on mine to cover my wedding band and got closer to me again for a kiss. The audience gave us a round of applause and waited eagerly for us to kiss each other, but I refused.

AN OLD LADY CAME TO US

At this time, an old lady who was in the crowd came to us. She said, "What a great performance. It's so good to see that you are so in love. You remind me of the loving relationship that I had with my husband."

Cristina said, "He is my life. Without him, life is meaningless to me. He is my inspiration to move forward. He is my everything."

I told the old lady, "You look so familiar. I feel like we've met before."

The old lady said, "Yes…you look familiar too." At this time, she took off the mask that was attached to her face and removed the fake gray hair from her head. It was Dr. Ann Ruby.

She then said, "You never, never come back to me again. You are my husband and are messing with this lady?! You dirty Secret Boyfriend! Get lost! Get lost! Get lost!" She walked angrily away.

Cristina collapsed on the ground. The audience was shocked and didn't know how to react. Just a few minutes ago, it was the most loving performance they had ever seen in their lives, and now this!!!

One lady in the group came to me and said, "I loved your dance with this lady. Would you be my Secret Boyfriend too?"

I yelled at her and said, "NOOOOO!"

Apparently, after the housekeeper told Dr. Ann Ruby I was giving baths to Cristina, washing her body, and putting on her panties and bra, she got suspicious and decided to follow us.

I lifted Cristina up and said, "We have to go. The walk will be a little uphill and a little harder."

She said, "I have no energy to walk. Will you carry me?"

I put her on my back, took her crutches, and started walking back to my car. People who were passing by looked at us a little strangely. I was walking with crutches and carrying a lady on my back!!!

An old couple in their eighties were walking by and saw us. The lady told her husband, who was walking with a cane, "This is real love. He bought her a flower and is now carrying her. You've never done that for me. Can you carry me on your back now, like them?"

The old man, who could barely walk, said, "Maybe when we go to heaven! We will start fresh, and I will carry you on my back, my love."

While I was carrying Cristina on my back, she was holding me in a very loving way. She turned her head and put it against my head. She kept the flower close to her face and kept kissing it. I was feeling her love was getting out of control…from my side too.

I took Cristina back to my car, then to her special facility building where she was living. I took her to her room, which was on the first floor facing the parking lot. I parked my car right in front of her room. I held her arm and helped her to walk to her room.

When the staff in the facility saw her, they all cheered and gave her a round of applause. They were surprised she could walk. They all came and gave her a hug.

I took her to her room and helped her to sit in the wheelchair, facing the window and looking at my car. I gave her a hug and left, even though I could feel she wanted a kiss from me; I controlled myself because I still wanted to be loyal to Dr. Ann Ruby.

I went outside to my car. Cristina was looking at me with a big smile and blew me a kiss. I moved my finger from left to right a few times and gave her the signal as if to say "no kiss," then showed her my wedding band.

She was disappointed but we both smiled at each other. I got into my car, and from the corner of my eye, I saw her holding the flower I had bought for her, kissing it again. She was far from breaking away from me. Unfortunately, I was enjoying that tremendously. Honestly, my love for Cristina had never died.

The new Cristina had become the true angel I had been looking for. I was looking for opportunities to do more for her because the rewards of her being thankful were so sweet and gave me the energy to go out of my way and do even more for her.

If she'd had this quality while we were together, we would never have had a marriage problem. We would probably have lived together for eternity.

I really loved the new Cristina. My love for her was getting out of control. I was falling dangerously in love with her. At the same time, I was dedicated to my wife, Dr. Ann Ruby. I absolutely did not want to lose her.

I WAS IN TROUBLE WITH DR. ANN RUBY

My idea was to put flowers and "I Love You" balloons in her office at the hospital. I wanted it to be done in the evening or in the very early morning while she was not in the hospital. I found a flower shop that was available that evening, so I drove directly to it.

They didn't have many flowers and I would have to buy more in the early morning. The plan was to decorate her office, outside her office, and the doctor/nurse station with lots of elegant flowers and balloons. And, of course, I had to pay them extra because it would be done very early in the morning.

Because of what had happened, I had decided not to sleep at home. I sent a message saying, "Sweetheart, my ONLY love, because of the unpleasant event that happened today, I better not sleep at home for tonight. I rented a hotel room."

Later, I texted her the name of the hotel and my room number. I then continued, "Let's meet tomorrow so I can explain. Remember, you are still my ONLY love. I will do anything in the world—if needed, I will bring Heaven and Earth together—so I can live every day of my life with you.

"If I hurt you, I apologize profusely, but it's not what you think it is. Please, give me a chance to explain it to you. I love you to death, babe! I will leave my phone on tonight for you. Please text or call me anytime you want. Or even come to my hotel room. Whatever you want, babe. Good night, my ONLY love. I am going to sleep now."

I woke up early the next morning and went to the flower market to pick up the best flowers, then went directly to the hospital to help arrange the flowers before she arrived to work. The whole thing was done before 7 a.m.

The day before, I had confirmed her schedule to make sure that we would finish before she got to work. Everything was done first-class. I wanted to impress her and melt her heart.

The night before, as I had expected, there had been no text or call. It had been calm and quiet. I had a feeling that it was the calm before a big and violent storm.

When she arrived, she was surprised to see the flowers and balloons all over the place at the doctor/nurse station and in her office. It was so impressive!

Suddenly, she lost control, picked up a surgical knife, and hit and burst every balloon, yelling, "I hate you…I hate you…I hate you! Get lost…get lost… get lost!" All the doctors and nurses went to that area to see what was going on, and so did some patients.

At the same time, someone on the intercom announced, "Dr. Ann Ruby…Dr. Ann Ruby…there is a stroke patient coming in. She is in bad shape and a mother of four. Her husband is begging us to save her life. Dr. Ann Ruby, you are the only one in the hospital now who could possibly reverse her stroke. Please get ready! She will be arriving shortly."

But Dr. Ann Ruby was busy bursting all the balloons and destroying all the flowers. More and more people were coming to that area to watch her show.

She took the knife and put it to her throat to cut and kill herself. Some blood was dripping from the tip of the knife.

They announced on the intercom again, "Dr. Ann Ruby…Dr. Ann Ruby…the patient will be here shortly. You are the only one in the hospital now who can treat her, and we have to act quickly."

But Dr. Ann Ruby had no plan to save her. She wanted to take her own life by cutting her throat.

The hospital called the police to see if they could help. Shortly after they arrived, prepared to get involved, the head of the department asked them to stay out of it and let them handle it.

The ambulance arrived and they took the patient to the emergency room. But Dr. Ann Ruby was trying to take her own life, right in front of her colleagues and co-workers.

The husband of the patient found out Dr. Ann Ruby was the only one who could save his wife. He went to her and fell to his knees, begging, "Dr. Ann Ruby, I have four children at home, one with special needs. I beg you…I beg you…please save my wife. If she becomes paralyzed, we don't know how to survive. I beg you…please save my wife."

Dr. Ann Ruby looked at him and seemed like she was getting out of that suicidal thinking. The husband got back on his feet and grabbed her medical uniform, holding it open with both hands so she could wear it. The silence was deafening. Everyone was waiting to see what would happen.

He repeated, "We have four children at home, one with special needs. We don't know how to survive. Please save her. Please save her…I beg you…please save her. Pleeeeease."

Dr. Ann Ruby looked at him and seemed a little numb. She was between pushing the surgical knife into her throat and saving his wife.

Everyone was quiet in the room. The police team stood behind the other people, and that would have been a great moment to arrest her and avoid a painful suicide of cutting her own throat in front those people, but the head of the department had insisted the police not take any action.

Since she knew Dr. Ann Ruby, she had a feeling that the tragedy could be avoided in a peaceful manner. She did not want the police to get involved at all.

As the husband was holding Dr. Ann Ruby's uniform for her to wear, the lady on the intercom announced again, "Dr. Ann Ruby...Dr. Ann Ruby... the patient is here. She desperately needs you."

Then the head of the department gave a signal for everyone to be completely quiet. Dr. Ann Ruby looked at the husband holding her uniform and begging her to save his wife. At the same time, she had the knife pushing at her throat and blood was dripping. She looked at the husband in a numb way.

It was a big gamble for the head of the department to ask the police not to get involved. Imagine if her suicide attempt was successful. The news would be devastating, all over Las Vegas.

"The top stroke specialist doctor in Las Vegas cut her own throat in the hospital, right in front of her colleagues, co-workers, and patients. Her husband is the top land developer in Las Vegas. It happened because she caught her husband with another lady, cheating on her. Guess with whom?! With his ex-wife, who is also a Filipina!"

She slowly put the surgical knife on the counter and put her arms inside the uniform the husband was holding for her.

Suddenly, everyone in the room erupted in joy, screaming, clapping, and clapping even more. It seemed like the happiest moment they'd had in that hospital.

Her co-worker, Dr. Fedelyn, who had attended her wedding, was there too. She ran to her and stopped the bleeding on her neck so she could go and take care of the patient. She also put the stethoscope around Dr. Ann Ruby's neck.

While everyone was still clapping, Dr. Ann Ruby closed her eyes, took a deep breath, and walked with confidence to where the patient was.

After several hours of tests and reviewing the results, Dr. Ann Ruby talked to the patient and husband. She said, "You had a stroke, but you are very lucky. It didn't do much damage. There is a big possibility much of it can be reversed. We will keep you here for forty-eight more hours to monitor you. You need to go to physical therapy, change your diet, and exercise. You must completely change your lifestyle. We will give you all the instructions. I have no doubt that, with the unconditional love of your husband, you will be able to reverse much of the damage."

As Dr. Ann Ruby was leaving the room, she turned again to the lady and said, "You are lucky to have a husband like him who loves you and is loyal to you so unconditionally. He saved your life…and mine, too."

The husband told Dr. Ann Ruby, "Thank you for saving my wife's life."

Dr. Ann Ruby went and hugged him and said, "No, thank YOU for saving my life first."

Dr. Ann Ruby took a break and went to the garden of the hospital. She felt great that by changing her hatred toward me, she was able to save someone's life. She felt so great.

She texted me and said, "Thank you for the beautiful flowers and balloons. I wasn't expecting them at all. They inspired me and it resulted in saving someone's life. I don't hate you anymore, because I strongly believe forgiveness is the key to ultimate happiness. Whenever you are ready, I am willing to talk to you and hear your side of the story. Love, your wife, hopefully FOREVER!"

I replied, "Sure…thanks. I love you, babe."

SEPARATING FROM DR. ANN RUBY

After work, Dr. Ann Ruby went home to rest and share her accomplishment with me, but instead, she was shocked when she saw the tent and portable toilet on the front lawn. I had put my small table and chair next to it and was working on my laptop.

She asked me, "What's going on?"

I said, "This is where I will be working and sleeping for the next thirty days."

She said, "What?! This is a prestigious neighborhood. You can't do this. The homeowner's association and the neighbors won't allow that. Why do you want to sleep here?"

I said, "I want to punish myself. I hurt you deeply. I hurt the love of my life sooo deeply. It's not what you think it is, but I still decided to punish myself. I don't deserve to sleep next to you in our home, so I've decided to sleep in this tent for thirty days until you forgive me. I still have the key to the house and will come inside to get my clothes and personal items as needed, but before I enter, I will contact you and get your permission."

She said, "Okay, I forgive you now. Please get rid of this tent and portable toilet and come inside. This is very embarrassing."

I said, "Thank you for your forgiveness, but I still want to punish myself. I will sleep in this tent and will run my business on my laptop right here."

Dr. Ann Ruby had come home to relax and celebrate her victory of overcoming the crisis in the hospital. She was so proud of herself. But instead, she found her husband living in a tent. She thought the morning crisis in the hospital was the worst she had ever seen, but the crisis of her husband sleeping in the tent right in front of their mansion was worse.

She had no idea how to solve this crisis. This was a lot worse than catching her husband with his ex-wife, Cristina, cheating on her. Her life had gone from bad to worse to out of control.

The neighbors quickly noticed the tent and reported it to the security guard of the subdivision. They immediately came to our house and asked me to remove the tent and the portable toilet.

They told me, "This is a very prestigious and high-class community. You can't have them here. In fact, some neighbors complained, and that's why we are here."

I told them, "There is nothing in the homeowner association's rules that prevents me from doing this. I am a land developer and I know it for a fact. They cannot force me to remove them. They must have a meeting and change the rules. By that time, I will be out because I am only planning to be here for thirty days."

119

Soon, the neighbors noticed me sleeping in the tent and came to take pictures and post them online. The news media heard about it and came to write reports about it. They brought their trailers and camped in front of our home. The local, national, and even international news stations reported on it.

The news said, "The top land developer in Las Vegas is sleeping in a tent in front of his home. Apparently, he cheated on his Filipina wife, who is the top stroke doctor in Las Vegas. Interestingly enough, his company developed this high-end, mansion-style subdivision. Now, he has been kicked out of his home in the subdivision they created."

The news helicopters were flying over our home to report this juicy news around the world. Among the news media, there was one from India World News, and Philippines International Juicy News, and of course, all national television networks like ABC, NBC, and even CNN International.

They were watching every move I was making in the tent, going to the portable toilet, and working on my laptop. My wife, Dr. Ann Ruby, is a conservative Filipina lady. I am sure she was not comfortable with all the attention we were getting.

The Indian reporter came near my tent and reported this with a very heavy Indian accent: "This is Vijendra with the India World News, reporting from Las Vegas. This news can only be found in Las Vegas.

"The Las Vegas top land developer has been kicked out of his home; apparently, he cheated on his Filipina wife. And listen to this, he was fooling around with his ex-wife...haha...who was also a Filipina.

"My question is, if your ex-wife was good, why did you divorce her in the first place? Another question, why are you sleeping in the tent? Las Vegas is the capital city of the most beautiful young ladies in the world. Go and find one and sleep in the penthouse of a nice hotel that you own."

Then the reporter from Philippines International Juicy News said, "This is Koomcha, reporting from Las Vegas. A Filipina wife caught her husband, a famous land developer, cheating on her. Guess with who? With his ex-wife, who is also a Filipina!

"She kicked him out of the house, which actually belongs to the husband. The husband is sleeping in the tent, begging his Filipina wife to go back to him.

"Why is he sleeping in the tent and begging his wife? Get a ticket and go to the Philippines. As soon as you get out of the airport, there are beautiful young ladies waiting for foreigners to marry them.

"Stay in the Philippines for two weeks, the ladies will take care of you like a king, with love and caring like you never experienced in the past. Choose one of them, marry her, and bring her here to the US.

"But don't let them become independent and don't let them get their US passports. Because if they do, some of them will run away.

"But that's okay. If they run away, you can go back again to the Philippines and bring another fresh and young one."

Dr. Ann Ruby couldn't take the activities anymore. She called me and said, "I need to talk to you immediately. This must end. How about tomorrow morning, eleven a.m. in the park next to the hospital?"

I agreed.

In the morning, she got ready, got into her car, opened the garage door, and drove away to drop off our children first, then go to work. The reporters immediately noticed her and ran to her car.

Even though her windows were all up and closed, they asked her very loudly, "Dr. Ann Ruby, Dr. Ann Ruby, where did you catch your husband cheating on you? In the master bedroom, taking a shower together, or having sex on the kitchen island? Were they both nude?" She did not pay attention to them and sped away.

Later, she texted me and said, "Since we are being followed, meeting in the park is not safe. Come to the second floor, the conference room is on your right. We'll still meet at 11 a.m." I agreed with that. It was a smart idea.

When we met, we both smiled and lightly hugged each other. Before she said anything, I apologized for hurting her. I said, "Before we got married, I loved you so much and I still do. I promised myself I wouldn't do anything to hurt you. I am ashamed of myself that I hurt you, but it's not what you think it is."

She said, "What do you mean, it's not what I think it is? The housekeeper told me you personally give her a bath, wash her body, dry her body, and put on her panties and bra. These are totally unnecessary. She is not your wife anymore. She is your ex-wife. They have staff in that facility that can do it for her. Her hands are perfectly fine. Why were you putting on her bra?"

I said, "It's not what you think it is."

She said, "What? Seriously!!! How about that romantic dance with her, right in front of everyone in the park! And right in front of me too. Do you understand how painful it was for me to watch that? I have never seen that much love between a couple. I think you are deeply in love with her. She hurt you sooo much by running away with her Secret Boyfriend, she made our wedding a bloody one, but you still love her deeply. I wish you loved me like that."

She then continued, "I think you two should marry again."

I screamed, "What?! No way…I am loyal and committed to you. I will never leave you."

She laughed and said, "Loyal and committed to me and then putting a bra on your ex-wife?! No way, I am not interested. I want a divorce. I am serious. On top of that, if I stay in this marriage, I must fight with Angelina and Cristina, because both of them are interested in you, but if you marry Cristina, Angelina won't be after you anymore. I am done with this marriage. I am leaving."

DR. ANN RUBY Became a Lesbian

She then said, "Paul, I want to share a secret with you. I am a lesbian. I have always had this feeling, but because my beloved American ex-husband was so nice to me, I never expressed it and never told him."

Surprised, I said, "What? You are a lesbian?!"

She said, "Yes, you made me a lesbian."

I said, "What do you mean? How could I make you a lesbian? I am totally confused. Tell me about it!"

She said, "I have always been a lesbian. But because my ex-husband loved me so much, I controlled myself and was loyal to him. When you and I were together, during the last two months of his life, and then one year after that, I fell in love with you as a friend, it was mainly because we didn't sleep together, just holding hands, light hugging, and walking.

"But when we got married and went on our two-week honeymoon, I found out that marriage with you wasn't for me. You are too hot in the bed, having sex every night…every night…every night, and sometimes twice a night. You are like a firecracker and it was torture for me.

"It was clear to me that life wasn't for me. It was a matter of time for me to get out of the closet and live the life I want. I want to have my own wife. I want to be the husband of the family. Wearing these wedding rings is torturous. I want to return them to you. They're too girly and not for me." She took them off her finger and gave them to me.

I was shocked when I heard that. I didn't know how to react. She said, "You and your ex-wife, Cristina, are a perfect match. You should marry her again. I see both of you are sooo deeply in love. It seems to me your love for her never died, and it doesn't seem as if it ever will."

She continued, "On top of that, she is totally depending on you for recovery. Your unconditional love and support will give her the energy that she needs to recover. Otherwise, she will be disabled, maybe for life."

I really was shocked and had no idea how to react. If she really was a lesbian and wanted to have her own wife, that wouldn't be a good marriage for either of us. I had to let her go and support her however I could.

I said, "I am so shocked about what you said. In respect for each other, let's give each other one month to think about it. I promise you my relationship with Cristina will be professional, not washing her body and not putting on her bra. I will be a pure trainer.

"You also promise not to have any relationship with a potential future wife. We respect each other for one month, and then at the end of the month, we meet again and finalize our lives together." She agreed to that, and we hugged each other. I told her, "I will not sleep in the house. That will be my punishment for hurting you."

Before we left, she asked me, "Paul, I want to ask you something. After all she did to you, why do you still love her and why are you so committed to helping her?"

I said, "I don't love her, but I am very committed to her. It's because I feel I have unfinished business to complete. When we got married, my life was a mess. During the crash of the housing market in 2008, I lost my home-building company.

"In a short time, I went from Hero to Zero. If it weren't for Cristina, I wouldn't have got back on my feet. It took me several years, slowly but surely. I owe it to her. I must pay her back. I was actually looking for an opportunity to pay her back. This is the opportunity to help her so that she gets back on her feet, too."

I continued, "I think it's better to give ourselves a one-month break. Then we talk." I left the conference room and went back to my office in the tent.

Later that day, she came back from work. She parked her car in the garage and came to say hi to me. I was shocked when I saw her. She looked so different.

She had got a new haircut, which was very short. She said, "After I got the haircut, I went back to the hospital and told everyone that it's time for me to get out of the closet. I told everyone that I am a lesbian and want to have a wife."

Everyone was shocked too, but they wished her the best. She told them that we had decided to be husband and wife for another month, and then we would finalize it.

With her quick and bold action, she was telling me not to waste my time by waiting for her anymore. She wanted me to move on with Cristina and marry her. However, as I had promised to her, I decided not to make any decisions for one month.

I continued my training with Cristina and told her what had happened between Dr. Ann Ruby and me, and how our marriage was in such trouble. But I also told her that I was still very committed to helping her until she got back on her feet.

"But I want you to help me and do your best to make this process faster," I said, and she did give me the promise.

Our training continued and we were walking more and more, almost running. It was time to work on her speech. We were attending speech therapy together. There were some improvements but not many. My plan was to help her become a public speaker. I wanted her to share her amazing story of comeback with others and inspire her audiences.

She had no idea what my plan was. Being a conservative Filipina, standing and speaking in front of others would be the last thing in the world she wanted to do, especially with her new speech impediment. It seemed to be impossible.

I said, "Cristina, if you want to overcome your challenge of speaking, you have to accept one hundred percent responsibility for your speaking too, the way that you accepted responsibility for your walking. Doctors in both the Philippines and Las Vegas confirmed that there is no damage to your speaking mechanism. You just have to accept responsibility, even though it's not your fault."

I started teaching her how to stand behind the lectern and slowly practice public speaking. She was getting better and better. A week passed by, and we were progressing, day by day, slowly but surely.

I was still punishing myself for hurting Dr. Ann Ruby by sleeping in the tent. At the same time, I was missing her so badly. I seriously wanted to get back with her, but if she wanted to be a lesbian and have a wife, then I had to respect her wishes and see what was good for her.

What was troubling me was that when she was my girlfriend thirteen years ago, I never thought she could be a lesbian. She had been as girly as she could get. And when we were dating after her husband passed away, she was as sweet as she could be. She was the true love of my life, and I was praying that what I had heard from her was a bad dream, not true, and we could get back together.

I texted her regularly and asked her if there was anything I could do for her and the children, and she did ask me for favors a few times.

One time, the master bathroom sink needed some work. I took my tools, went upstairs, and fixed it. While I was there, I noticed that my picture was still on the nightstand next to her bedside, plus our wedding picture. That gave me some hope.

130

After one week of strange and painful separation, I asked her if we could meet for a coffee. She agreed. She asked me to meet at the park next to the hospital. She bought coffee and some pastries. It was a friendly meeting, and we did not talk about the details of our divorce. She looked at my wedding band, which I was still wearing. She could see and feel how committed I was to her.

After one week of dedicated training with Cristina, it was time to talk to her seriously. I said, "Cristina, I am fully committed to helping you get back on your feet, but because of that, my marriage is falling apart. I am fully committed to Dr. Ann Ruby, and I don't want to lose her. I am still fully committed to helping you and always will be, until your full recovery. But you have to find a boyfriend and come to our training with him."

Cristina became very angry at me and said, "That is a slap in the face. You are telling me to go and find a boyfriend by tomorrow?! You have no respect for me. You are treating me like a slave! You are disgusting!!! Because I am disabled and need you, it doesn't mean that you can tell me anything you want. You help me and I appreciate that, but at the same time, you hurt me so badly."

I said, "The fact is, I can no longer see you alone. My marriage is falling apart because I am helping you. You either find a boyfriend and come with him, or I cannot see you anymore. You have to find a boyfriend in twenty-four hours; otherwise, tomorrow, I will not come."

She said, "The only way to find a boyfriend in twenty-four hours is to hire a Secret Boyfriend like you."

I replied, "That may not be a bad idea either. Do whatever you can."

She said, "Actually, there is a doctor who comes to our facility, and he likes me. He is divorced and single and has one kid. I never showed any interest in him because I love you so much and was hoping that we could get married and have the same wedding that you had with Dr. Ann Ruby. That would be a dream wedding…with you, of course.

"But I can clearly see you are so committed to Dr. Ann Ruby, and I have to accept the fact this will not happen. I cannot take the chance of not seeing you anymore because that will be more torturous for me."

She continued, "That doctor in the hospital gave me his cell number and asked me to go out for coffee. I am going to call him and accept his invitation. Maybe he can come with me to our trainings. Paul, you are a good man and I don't want to ruin your marriage. I would rather see you as a friend than not see you at all."

I was in the middle of my painful separation with Dr. Ann Ruby. I could feel she was being nicer to me by texting me. I knew her well, and I could feel behind her texts the love was coming back, but maybe as a friend only.

As the first year after the passing of her husband, she asked to have a heart-to-heart relationship, not even holding hands. I decided to use the same approach, not push her, and to let her make the first move.

One time, she called me and said our two sons had been playing in their room and had pushed against the closet doors, and one door had fallen off. She asked me if I could fix it. I took my tools and went to the house.

After fixing the closet door, since no one was at home, I went to the master bedroom to see if my picture was still on the nightstand next to her side, or if it had been replaced by a picture of her future wife.

When I went to the master bedroom, I could not believe what I saw. She had put my picture on an iPad, and put it next to her pillow, facing her, so she could see me while in bed. The iPad was on. She probably left it on twenty-four seven. I hadn't been expecting that at all. I was so confused and couldn't put the pieces of the puzzle together.

If she had decided to become a lesbian and have a wife, then why was my picture next to her pillow?! It was a great feeling, but I didn't want to be too optimistic. I loved her so much that if she wanted to have a wife, I was ready and determined to support her.

She became a lot nicer to me and invited me to come sleep in the guest room of our home, but I refused and stayed in my tent. Every time she came home, after parking her car in the garage, if I was working in the tent, she would come and say hi to me.

The first thing she always looked at was my wedding band, which I was still wearing twenty-four seven. Even though she said she wanted to have her own wife, I was still committed to helping her until the end of our one month so we could finalize our relationship.

Cristina called me and said she was ready to bring her new boyfriend to our training. It was welcome news. We met the next day, and she introduced Dr. Craig to me. We chatted a little bit. He was a very nice and enjoyable man.

Apparently, Cristina had told him about our past. He thanked me for my dedication to helping Cristina, even as it had put my own marriage in danger.

We started our regular morning walk, then had a power walk, and a little uphill. It was taking lots of energy for Cristina, who had only recently learned to walk again.

Dr. Craig was very helpful and enjoying Cristina's perseverance. At the end, Dr. Craig thanked me for helping her.

The next day, Cristina bought a bouquet of flowers, and with Dr. Craig, her new boyfriend, went to the hospital to see Dr. Ann Ruby. Dr. Craig checked her schedule and knew when she was going to work. They waited in the parking lot until she arrived, then they went to her car. Dr. Craig had met Dr. Ann Ruby a few times, so they knew each other. Cristina introduced Dr. Craig as her new boyfriend.

Dr. Ann Ruby was delighted to hear the news. Cristina told Dr. Craig, "Honey, I'd like to have a few minutes of private time with Dr. Ann Ruby." He went back to his car.

Cristina gave the bouquet of flowers to Dr. Ann Ruby and said, "I am really, really sorry if I hurt you. It was all my fault. While helping me, Paul always had his wedding band on. He said several times how committed and loyal he is to you. It was me who encouraged him to get closer to me. What I did was totally inappropriate.

"A few days ago, Paul told me that he no longer wants to work with me alone. He said because of training me, his marriage is falling apart. He said he will still train me, but I must find a boyfriend and bring him with me. He has to be there the whole time."

She laughed lightly and said, "He basically forced me to find a boyfriend. In the past, Dr. Craig, who was working part-time in our facility and visiting me, showed some interest toward me and invited me to go out for coffee. He even gave me his private cell number.

"A couple of days ago, I called him and accepted his invitation. He was delighted and we had our first date the same evening. It was a lot better than I was expecting. I briefly told him my story and asked him if he could come to training with me since Paul was getting busy and may not be able to continue with me.

"Dr. Craig immediately and joyfully accepted my offer and said, 'It means we will be dating while we are in therapy too.' Over the last two days, Paul worked with me while Dr. Craig was with me."

Dr. Ann Ruby was totally surprised, seeing her walking so well. She said, "It's a miracle. What happened?! A few days ago, you were in a wheelchair."

Cristina said, "It's all because of your husband and my strong love for him. I was willing to do anything for him, even though I knew it was a wrong love. I swear to God, during all those times, Paul never kissed me, even though I had a strong desire to kiss him. His dedication to you is solid."

She continued, "I truly apologize for my behavior. I am sorry if I hurt you. Please forgive me. I beg you to forgive me. Luckily, I have a new boyfriend who loves me to death." She laughed again and said, "Thanks to your husband, who forced me to have a boyfriend."

Dr. Ann Ruby hugged Cristina tightly and accepted her request for forgiveness. It was very emotional. They both cried tears of joy.

When Dr. Craig saw them, he came out of his car, smiling at that joyful moment. Dr. Ann Ruby looked at Dr. Craig and said, "Welcome to our family," and hugged him too. Then they left.

Later, Cristina called me and told me everything to make me happy. She said, "I did that so that I could bring you and Dr. Ann Ruby back together."

I said, "Cristina, thank you very much. It was very nice of you to do that. But it may be too late because Dr. Ann Ruby said she wants to get out of the closet and become a lesbian. She wants to have a wife and be the husband of the family."

Cristina was shocked to hear that and almost collapsed. She said, "I noticed her hairstyle is different. I got a little suspicious, but I thought maybe she just wanted to have a change in style."

She continued, "Wow…it's a big surprise…totally unexpected. So, what are you going to do? I want to tell you that my relationship with Dr. Craig is right at the very beginning. We are trying to learn about each other."

She laughed and said, "I had no plans to have a boyfriend. I did it because you forced me to have one; otherwise, I couldn't see you anymore. I am still fully in love with you, Paul, and would be delighted to get back with you."

I said, "NO, absolutely NOT! I want you to focus on Dr. Craig. He is a good man and cares for you a lot. I want the relationship between us to be like two best friends for life. I am still very committed to Dr. Ann Ruby. Even if she wants to have a wife, I will support her fully."

Cristina said, "Then, what are you going to do? You will be alone."

I said, "Don't worry. I am a professional Secret Boyfriend. I can find another quickly." We both laughed.

My training with Cristina continued, with Dr. Craig being with her at all the sessions. He seemed to be deeply in love with her, and I felt Cristina had the same feelings toward him as well.

We started walking more, power walking, running, and hiking. I felt the love of Dr. Craig was giving her the energy to do better and to impress him, but Dr. Craig was already impressed with her walking situation.

We resumed her training to be a public speaker so that she could share her amazing story of comeback with others and lift them up. That was something I was adamant I could help her with.

At the beginning, she was very resistant. She said, "Paul, I can hardly say my name in front of a group. I would rather die than speak in front of people. I don't want to be disrespectful to you, but don't even try. It will be a total waste of your time."

It seemed to me Dr. Craig was more interested in learning to speak in public than Cristina. I said, "Cristina, we start easy. The first lesson is when you come and stand in front of people, you must imagine you own the place. They are all on your property. This will build up your confidence and help you tremendously."

I said, "The first thirty seconds of the presentation is the most important part of your speech. If you don't get the attention of your audience in the beginning, you will have a hard time getting it later."

Dr. Craig was really paying attention to what I was saying and asked me if he could also practice in front of me. He had to give presentations at work and it had always been a challenge for him.

He said, "If I could talk in front of people and colleagues and give presentations, I would have excelled in my career."

After a few days, they were both improving, but Dr. Craig took it more seriously. He was actually coaching Cristina, too.

SURPRISE ENDING?!

My one-month separation with Dr. Ann Ruby was coming to an end. We were still friends, and I was going into the house to take care of a few things as needed. I told Cristina the date for our last day of our separation. It was on a Saturday.

I asked her to invite Dr. Ann Ruby and me for a hiking trip to celebrate her amazing progress. She gladly agreed.

She called Dr. Ann Ruby and invited her and said I was coming too. Dr. Ann Ruby gladly accepted the invite. The weather was beautiful and romantic.

I asked Dr. Ann Ruby if I could give her a ride so she wouldn't be alone. She agreed, so I picked her up with my white Mercedes convertible. The weather was nice, and we were cruising on the road. It created a very romantic driving experience. We were talking like two friends, and with some laughing too.

We met at the parking lot of Red Rock Canyon in Las Vegas. Cristina and Dr. Craig had arrived a little earlier and were waiting for us. They were leaning against Dr. Craig's car and hugging each other, with Cristina's head on his shoulder. We were surprised and, at the same time, so happy to see them so in love.

We got out of our car and Dr. Ann Ruby gave Cristina a bouquet of flowers she had bought for them. She congratulated them and said, "I am in the medical field. Your recovery is more than amazing. It's a miracle."

Cristina immediately replied, "Your husband gets all of the credit. If it weren't for him, I would still be in a wheelchair. I owe it all to your husband."

She had clearly said the words "your husband" and emphasized them, hoping the love would spark. But it was a wishful dream. There was absolutely no chance of us getting back together.

We started walking and hiking. We went a little faster and a little uphill. Dr. Craig and Cristina were walking in front of us, holding hands like two inseparable lovers, and we were right behind them.

Dr. Ann Ruby was shocked to see how Cristina had recovered so fast to almost normal.

Finally, we reached the top, with an astonishing view. We rested for a little bit, and then Dr. Craig asked me to take some pictures of him and Cristina.

He said, "I want to thank Cristina, as she has brightened my life. I also want to thank Paul for his unconditional love and support so Cristina could get back on her feet. Paul, Cristina and I will be eternally thankful to you."

He looked at Cristina and said, "I love you, baby. I love you with every fiber of my heart and soul. Thank you for coming into my life."

Unexpectedly, he bent down on one knee, took the engagement ring out of his pocket, and said, "Cristina, you are the love of my life. Will you marry me?"

It was *totally* unexpected. Cristina had no idea this would happen. She said, "Of course, of course, of course, my love. This is my dream come true." Dr. Craig gracefully put the ring on her finger. It was a beautiful moment to watch them so in love.

Having known Cristina for twelve years, I could feel deep down, she was very sad because she was the reason that Dr. Ann Ruby and I had separated. Today was our last day, and she was praying for a miracle.

DR. ANN RUBY: WHERE ARE MY RINGS?!

Dr. Ann Ruby then looked at me and said, "Where are my rings?"

I said, "What do you mean? You returned them to me and said you want to have a wife and be the husband of the family."

She said, "I lied to you. I thought you cheated on me, so I decided to hurt you the most. You know something, instead of hurting you, I hurt myself a lot more. Every night, it was torture for me not to hug you in bed. Instead, I was sleeping while hugging your picture. I was hoping before the end of our one-month separation, you would still be available so we could get back together."

She continued, "Cristina told me how committed you were to me the whole time. She said you even kept my rings in your pocket, close to your heart all the time. Cristina tried her hardest to get us back together."

She added, "At the same time, I have to say, Paul, you are a crazy man. Sometimes, you are beyond crazy, you are embarrassing, like putting the tent in our front yard and working and sleeping there. But you know something? I like a crazy husband. You are perfect for me.

"Paul, we both hurt each other a lot, but I strongly believe that FORGIVENESS is the key to ultimate happiness. Can I have my rings back, pleeeeease?"

I could not believe what I was hearing. I said, "Sure...sure..." I then took the rings out of my pocket and bent on one knee to say, "Dr. Ann Ruby, you are the love of my life. I don't think I can live without you. Will you be my wife...AGAIN... Pleeeeease?"

She screamed and said, "Yesss! Yesss! Yesss...of course!" I put the rings on her finger and she gave me a big hug and kiss.

At this time, Cristina suddenly jumped up and down and screamed, "Yesss...Yesss...Yesss..." It seemed like she was a lot more excited than Dr. Ann Ruby and me. She ran toward us and hugged and kissed both of us. She was very excited to see we were back together. In twelve years of being with Cristina, I had never seen her that happy.

Dr. Ann Ruby continued, "I want something else, too. If you can promise that to me, and right in front of Cristina and Dr. Craig, I will stay with you to my last breath."

I said, "Sure…anything. I will do anything for you. What do you want, my love?"

She said, "In addition to being my husband, I want you to be my Secret Boyfriend, too. Remember all those romantic texts you used to send to me while being my Secret Boyfriend? You were melting my heart. I want you to be my Secret Boyfriend again, but only MY Secret Boyfriend…my private Secret Boyfriend.

"Every day, I want you to send me those romantic messages again, like these:

'You are my everything! You are my world. The rest of the world is secondary.

'Remember, you are my ONLY love. I will do anything in the world—if needed, I will bring Heaven and Earth together—so I can be with you.

'Goodnight, my ONLY love.'"

Cristina said, "Listen to this text from Paul: 'My love, I will do anything to melt your heart because you are my ONLY love.'" They laughed.

146

Dr. Craig got a little jealous and raised his voice and said, "What?! Paul sent that to you?"

Cristina said, "Honey, why have you become jealous? At that time, you were not even in my life.

"And always remember that it was Paul who forced me to be your girlfriend and go out with you. And after our first date, I couldn't stop; I wanted to have more and more. I wanted to have all of you. Finally, today, you gave me all of you. So, we should both be very thankful to Paul."

We left that beautiful mountaintop. All four of us were super happy we were going to start our new lives. Cristina said to Dr. Craig, "I'd like our wedding to be the same as Paul and Dr. Ann Ruby's wedding, and in the same hotel in Davao City, Philippines. My love, can we afford it?"

Dr. Craig said, "My love, I will do anything to melt your heart because you are my ONLY love."

We all laughed, and Cristina said, "Sweetheart, you are a fast learner."

Cristina looked at Dr. Craig and said, "Honey, at our wedding, after I've danced with you, I want to dance with Paul. Will that be okay with you, my love?"

Dr. Craig immediately and without any hesitation said, "Yes, of course. We are all part of one happy family now."

WE SAID GOODBYE TO REPORTERS?!

When we went home, the TV reporters were still parked in front of our home. They were surprised I had picked up my lesbian wife and gone out. By the way we were dressed, it was obvious we had been on a date.

I parked my car in the garage and Dr. Ann Ruby took my hand, then we both walked toward the reporters. Dr. Ann Ruby said to the reporters, "I'd like to make an announcement."

Suddenly, all the microphones came toward us. Dr. Ann Ruby turned toward me, put her hands around my head, and gave me a long and juicy kiss in front of those reporters. She turned to them and said, "I have no more announcements. Bye!" She took my hand and we walked toward the front door of our home.

The reporters, yelling and screaming, asked, "Dr. Ann Ruby...Dr. Ann Ruby...we heard you became a lesbian and wanted to have a wife. How about that?!"

Dr. Ann Ruby turned her head toward the reporters and said, "I lied…I fooled you guys." She opened the door of our home, took my hand, pulled me inside, and locked the door behind us.

The reporters were confused and disappointed. They thought the news was getting juicier and juicier, but instead, it had a quick and happy ending. They didn't want to have a happy ending. They wanted it to be juicier so they could entertain their audiences.

After some romantic time at home, Dr. Ann Ruby and I went outside and took down the tent and brought all my things into the garage. The reporters kept filming us and asking us questions, but we completely ignored them.

We cleaned the front yard and went back inside our home. When the reporters saw the happy ending was really the end, they slowly packed up their equipment and left.

The neighbors were excited to see that all the reporters were finally gone. I ordered a big banner that said, "We Are Happily Back Together," and I put it on the garage door. It was hard to miss. The neighbors saw that, and all came with flowers and congratulated us. The whole neighborhood was full of joy to see us back together, but more than that, to see that there was no tent in our front yard.

I called the florist who had done the flower arrangement for Dr. Ann Ruby last time. I asked her if she could do the same thing at her office. I said, "I know it's on short notice, and early morning is an inconvenience. I will pay you extra. She goes to work at eight a.m. Make sure everything is done before her arrival."

She said, "It's very short notice, but I think we can handle it."

I asked her, "Do you need me to be there?"

She said, "No, I know exactly what you want. It will be done before she arrives."

The next morning, Dr. Ann Ruby woke up excited. We were both ready to re-start our new life. She put on her nice dress and lovely makeup, put on her rings, and went to work. She looked so sexy and elegant, especially with that short hair. She looked like a model that had just walked off of a fashion show stage.

The flower arrangements were done on time. When her colleagues and co-workers arrived, they were scared to see them, as they remembered what had happened last time.

Dr. Ann Ruby arrived on time. When they saw her coming in like a model, they were surprised. She proudly showed her rings and said, "Hello, everyone. I got engaged over the weekend with the love of my life."

Someone asked, "Who is the lucky lady to be your wife?"

She proudly said, "I got re-engaged to my wonderful husband, Paul. We are happily back together."

The lady asked, "But you said you wanted to be a lesbian and have a wife?"

She said, "I lied. Paul hurt me so badly, I wanted to punish him and made up that story. I wanted to hurt him the most. Then I found out, I actually hurt myself the most. I realized I couldn't live without him. He did nothing wrong. It was a total misunderstanding."

She continued, "During the whole time, Paul was so committed to me and kept my wedding rings in his pocket close to his heart.

"On Saturday, it was the end of our one-month separation. We went out for a date to finalize our relationship. I was praying he hadn't fallen in love with another lady. When I found out he was still available, I immediately told him I wanted my rings back before someone else stole him from me.

"He could not believe that. He gladly put them on my finger. Now we are both super excited. We both realized we mean a lot to each other and cannot live without each other."

Everyone in her department was so excited to see us back together.

CRISTINA'S WEDDING

Cristina and Dr. Craig were very serious and deeply in love. They wanted to have their wedding soon, and they did. They decided to have it in the same place Dr. Ann Ruby and I had our wedding…the Grand Ballroom of the Marco Polo Hotel in Davao City, Philippines. The same place where she had tried to commit suicide.

They invited almost the same people who were at our wedding. This time, Angelina's husband, Mark, attended too. And, of course, Dr. Ann Ruby and I were invited.

The guests were so amazed to see Cristina was walking normally and talking almost perfectly. Cristina wanted to leave the painful suicide attempt in the past and start a new chapter. She wanted to do it in front of her family and friends.

They arranged a similar style of music and had twenty servers as dancers like our wedding. I helped her prepare her wedding speech. Since she had learned how to speak in front of people, she was very excited to give her wedding speech. It would be the speech of her life. She was very motivated and practiced a lot.

After the wedding, she danced with her new husband, Dr. Craig. Then, she asked me to dance with her. After the dance, she was ready to give the speech. She wanted to put her past behind her and start fresh with Dr. Craig, Dr. Ann Ruby, and me.

Before the wedding, Cristina bought a fake handgun. It looked like a real gun, made the sounds of a real gun, and after each fake shot, a little smoke came out of it.

The master of ceremonies announced, "Ladies and Gentlemen, please pay attention...please pay attention. The bride, Cristina, wants to say a few words. I also want to announce that the gun in her hand is a fake handgun. It's not real. Please give a big round of applause for Cristina."

Everyone started clapping and Cristina went to the middle of the stage. She waited until everyone was quiet. The silence was deafening.

She pulled out her fake gun and shot a couple of shots into the ceiling, like she had at our wedding.

She then put the fake gun into her mouth. The audience became scared, even though they knew it was fake.

She fired one shot into her mouth and fell on the floor. She waited for a few seconds. I went to her and offered my hand to lift her up. She stood and took a deep breath. I took her fake gun and gave her the microphone.

She took another deep breath, stood firmly, and said:

"Ladies and Gentlemen, it was in this very room, at the end of my beloved ex-husband's wedding with the lovely Dr. Ann Ruby, that I couldn't handle the jealousy and decided to make their wedding a bloody one. I did what you saw a few minutes ago. I was a sick person. I was beyond sick.

"Luckily, I survived, but I lost my ability to walk, and I could hardly talk. I was told I'd have to be in a wheelchair for life.

"When Paul and Dr. Ann Ruby came back from their honeymoon, they heard about this tragedy. They came directly to the hospital to see me. When I was hopeless, lying on my bed, when my Secret Boyfriend had dumped me and no one wanted me, Paul kindly took my hand.

"I told him I felt numbness in my right arm. He immediately started massaging my right arm and hand. It brought tears to my eyes and I could see a ray of light at the end of the dark tunnel.

"While he was sitting on my bed, the doctor came. She said, 'There is a slight chance she might regain her ability to walk and talk. But it can only be accomplished by her sheer determination, relentless therapy, and practice, and with the help of a super-dedicated husband, boyfriend, or a very loyal and committed BEST friend.' Then she left.

"Paul held my hand and said, 'Remember after our separation, I told you I want to be your BEST friend, but you never replied? Now, I want to ask you again: Cristina, I want to be your BEST friend…will you accept my offer?'

"I burst into tears again and could hardly talk. I said to him, 'Paul, you are an angel. With all I did to you, while I am helpless in this hospital bed, while I have no one in America to help me, you offer me this?! How could I not see that side of you?!'

"I told him, 'That suicide attempt completely changed my life because, from today, I want to be an angel like you and your wife, Dr. Ann Ruby. I want to become an emergency room nurse to save people's lives.'

"'Paul, thank you for being my BEST friend. Paul, will you stay with me as my BEST friend until I graduate?' He hugged me and said, 'YES, I will be your BEST friend all the way to the end.'

"Shortly after, we packed up our stuff and headed back to Las Vegas, USA. While his lovely wife was on one side, Paul was pushing my wheelchair. As my new and committed BEST friend, he was determined to push my wheelchair all the way to a full recovery.

"Only a true angel could do such a thing. He risked his marriage with Dr. Ann Ruby to help me get back on my feet.

"He started working religiously with me. It was during that time I met my beloved husband, whom I love dearly. He is my everything.

"Everyone thinks my recovery was a miracle. Yes, I also think it was a miracle. And this miracle happened because my beloved ex-husband extended his hand to me and said, 'I want to be your Best Friend. Will you accept my offer?' And, of course, I did.

"Ladies and Gentlemen…please stand up… Look at the person on your right, extend your hand, and say, I want to be your Best Friend. Will you accept my offer?

"Now, look at the person on your left, extend your hand, and say, I want to be your Best Friend. Will you accept my offer?

"Now, extend your hand to the people of the world and say it loudly. People of the world, I want to be your Best Friend. Will you accept my offer?"

Everyone was full of joy and clapping. Cristina and Dr. Craig started their final dance. Dr. Ann Ruby and I joined them dancing on the stage. Angelina and Mark followed us. Their mother could not control her emotions. She jumped on stage and danced with us and hugged everyone.

From the first day I met Cristina in Davao City, Philippines, my greatest joy was seeing her SHINE! That night...she was the STAR!

At the end of the wedding, Cristina came to me and whispered into my ear: "Paul, I have exciting news to share with you. So far, I have only told my husband. Paul, today, I found out that I am pregnant." She gave me a bear hug and kissed me on my cheek, leaving a lipstick mark with the imprint of her beautiful lips. That was the icing on the cake.

Finally, we became BEST friends.

I then sneaked out the back door, grabbed my laptop, ran to Starbucks, and got my venti dark-roast coffee. With Cristina's lipstick mark still on my cheek, I flew to space, sat on that rock, and started writing my next novel, *Secret Boyfriend, Part II*.

T   h   e   E   n   d

Paul Noor
From a rock in space above Las Vegas, USA
www.SecretBoyfriend.com

August, 2021

158

From the Author

Thank you for reading this novel. My intention was to turn my sad story into an entertaining and inspiring novel with **FORGIVENESS** at its core, and with a sweet ending of **Uniting Broken Relationships**. If you feel I have accomplished my goal, and if you enjoyed it, kindly write a positive review on Amazon.com. It would be the best compliment you could give to me.

About Paul Noor

I started my career as a Civil Engineer. After a few years of working as an engineering manager for a couple of companies, I started my own home-building company. In five years, I went from being in debt to a self-made millionaire. How did that happen? I had "a burning desire to get ahead, and then share my blessings with others."

While I was at the peak of my career, the 2008 crash of the housing market crushed my business, but not my spirit. I immediately got back on my feet and reinvented myself. I went "From Building Homes to Building Leaders"…training CEOs, presidents, executives, and employees of different companies.

However, my greatest achievement in life was my journey **From Stuttering to Motivational Speaking**.

When I was in college, my goal was to become a college professor. I finished all my PhD courses with straight As. Unfortunately, at that time, my stuttering had become so severe that learning sign language seemed to be the best option for me to communicate. My dream of becoming a college professor was completely shattered, but not my determination.

Over the next thirty years, with intensive speech therapy, relentless practice, and sheer determination, I gained control over my speech. Since then, I have spoken at numerous organizations, including Fortune-500 companies such as **Walt Disney**, **FedEx**, and **Lockheed Martin**. How did that happen?! I never never gave up on my **DREAM**!

What's your **DREAM**?

Paul Noor

Invite Paul to speak at your meetings and events.
His speeches are entertaining and inspiring.
www.SecretBoyfriend.com

I had a DREAM

I met **Pope Francis** and **Kim Jong Un** of North Korea.

A letter to my beautiful Filipina ex-wife:

Sweetheart, ever since I caught you with your Secret Boyfriend in his white Mercedes convertible, you went into hiding and left me hopeless in my red Honda Civic. I then wrote my novel, *Secret Boyfriend*, so that I could help and inspire others.

Last night, I had a DREAM that my novel did well. Then Walt Disney made a movie out of it, which did super well. I even played in the movie and won an Oscar.

After receiving the Oscar, while still on the stage, right in front of the world audience, I bent on one knee and proposed to the leading Filipina actress in the movie. She screamed and said, "YESSSSS!" I then put the engagement ring on her finger.

The people in the Philippines watched it live on their televisions as the event was unfolding. The whole country erupted in JOY. The jubilation lifted the whole nation.

Shortly after this, President Duterte of the Philippines invited us to meet with him. Soon, a parade was arranged for leading actors and me. Over a million people came to the streets to celebrate the victory. The jubilation lifted the whole Philippines.

Pope Francis heard about it. His Holiness invited me to go to the Vatican so we could watch the movie together. He enjoyed it tremendously and praised me for turning my sad story into an entertaining and inspiring novel with **FORGIVENESS** at its core, and with a sweet ending of **Uniting Broken Relationships**.

His Holiness asked me to become his peace messenger and go to North Korea and ask Kim Jong Un to get rid of his nuclear arsenals. Kim gladly agreed to do that.

While Kim and I were grilling together for a BBQ in his backyard, they were blowing up atomic bombs right in front of us, one by one. The whole world was watching it live on TV. The jubilation lifted the whole universe.

Kim and I became buddies and we both won Nobel Peace Prizes.

The novel and the movie made me a wealthy man. I then contacted you and said, "Sweetheart, I want to buy you a gift, a rental property in the Philippines for your retirement. But the condition is to become each other's BEST friend, and to meet once a week and hug each other."

You did not reply. I said, "I will buy two rental properties." You did not reply. I said, "Ten rental properties. Take it or leave it." You immediately replied, "YES…YES…I'll take it…I'll take it…"

For our first weekly hug, we met at the parking lot of the McDonald's on Las Vegas Blvd in front of the South Point Casino. We got out of our cars, hugged each other, and left.

It was the most expensive hug I have ever received from a lady, but it was worth it. Finally, we became BEST friends. The jubilation lifted everybody!

When I woke up from my dream, I said, "If my novel and the movie do well, and if I meet President Duterte, Pope Frances, and Kim Jong Un, I will buy those rental properties for you."

Sweetheart, please pray for that. Remember, your retirement depends on it too. **HUG!**

Paul Noor
I want to be your **BEST** Friend.
Will you accept my offer?

Secret Boyfriend — Paul Noor

Secret Boyfriend — Paul Noor

Secret Boyfriend — Paul Noor